SALOON SHOWDOWN

Clint turned, drawing his gun at the same time, dropping to one knee.

Doyle got off the first shot, but it went over Clint's head. Clint fired and saw his bullet strike the man in the right shoulder, high up. It spun him around and caused him to drop his gun, but Clint knew the shot wouldn't kill him. That was good. He needed one of them alive to say who had hired them. . . .

DON'T MISS THESE
ALL-ACTION WESTERN SERIES
FROM THE BERKLEY PUBLISHING GROUP

THE GUNSMITH by J. R. Roberts
Clint Adams was a legend among lawmen, outlaws, and ladies. They called him . . . the Gunsmith.

LONGARM by Tabor Evans
The popular long-running series about U.S. Deputy Marshal Long—his life, his loves, his fight for justice.

LONE STAR by Wesley Ellis
The blazing adventures of Jessica Starbuck and the martial arts master, Ki. Over eight million copies in print.

SLOCUM by Jake Logan
Today's longest-running action Western. John Slocum rides a deadly trail of hot blood and cold steel.

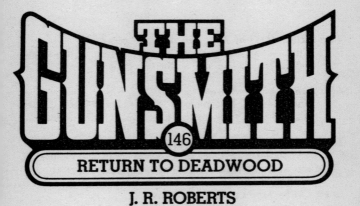

THE GUNSMITH

146

RETURN TO DEADWOOD

J. R. ROBERTS

JOVE BOOKS, NEW YORK

RETURN TO DEADWOOD

A Jove Book/published by arrangement with the author

PRINTING HISTORY
Jove edition/February 1994

ISBN: 0-515-11315-8

A JOVE BOOK®
Jove Books are published by The Berkley Publishing Group,
200 Madison Avenue, New York, New York 10016.
JOVE and the "J" design are trademarks belonging to Jove Publications, Inc.

PRINTED IN THE UNITED STATES OF AMERICA

10 9 8 7 6 5 4 3 2 1

ONE

Clint Adams had not been to Deadwood, South Dakota, since the death of his good friend Wild Bill Hickok at the hands of the coward, Jack McCall.

In fact, he had thought very little of Deadwood until that morning, when a letter had been delivered to his room at a very inopportune moment.

He was in Labyrinth, Texas, a town which he had come to think of as his base of operations, if not as his home. But he was still careful not to form any permanent ties there. Probably the closest thing he had to that was his friendship with Rick Hartman, the owner of the saloon and gambling establishment, Rick's Place. And while he did help himself from time to time to the women who worked for Rick, he had made a point of never letting any of them think he was looking

1

for anything other than some pleasant time spent together. For the most part, the girls—who came and went quite often—willingly went along with that arrangement.

The girl who was in his bed that morning had only worked for Rick for about a month. She was not even living in Labyrinth the last time Clint had been there. She had come to town and been hired in his absence. Now he had been back a week and had his eye on Lisa Wilkes for that whole time.

"Who's that?" he asked Rick on his first night back.

"That's Lisa Wilkes," Rick said. "How did I know you'd be interested?"

Lisa was tall and dark-haired. While she had a very small waist, she had full hips and breasts. Her skin was very pale and smooth. She liked to wear her black hair piled high on her head when she worked, which gave everyone an unobstructed view of her lovely, long neck.

"Did you know that when you hired her?" Clint asked.

"Yes," Rick said. "But I don't hire my girls because I think you'll like them. As it turns out, she's been very good for business."

"It's no wonder," Clint said.

"Three days."

"What?"

"I give it three days," Rick Hartman said, "and she's in your bed."

"What makes you say that?"

"She hasn't given a man a tumble in the month

she's been here," Rick said.

"So?"

"It's been my experience—my observation—that you appeal to women who have, oh, let's say . . . particular tastes in men."

"Is that a fact?"

"No, it's not," Rick said. "I told you, it's my observation."

"I didn't know you were such a student of human nature, Rick," Clint said, shaking his head.

"I know a little bit about people," Rick said. "You have to, in my business."

Well, Clint had to admit that Rick was very good at his business, so maybe he knew what he was talking about.

"Three days, huh?" he said.

"Three days," Rick said, nodding his head. "Starting right now."

As it turned out Rick Hartman had underestimated Clint. It only took two days. . . .

Now it was four days after that, and Lisa had warmed his bed all but one of them.

"I don't want to spoil you," she had told him on that particular night.

He'd smiled and left the saloon without her. If she thought that he was going to ask her again, she had another thing coming. It looked as if she was testing him that night, to see how he would take rejection. Apparently, she didn't like the easygoing way he'd reacted, because the next night *she* had asked *him* if she could come to his room with him. He'd been tempted then to tell her that *he* didn't want to spoil *her*, but he decided against it. It seemed to him that she had gotten the point on her own without him pounding it home further. He was *not* going to ask her more than once.

When the knock came at the door that morning, he had her warm body pressed tightly to his. His hands were on her buttocks, massaging them, and her mouth was on his neck. Her hands were roaming over his body, and when the knock came they both stopped.

"They'll go away," she said, into his ear.

He pressed his nose to her neck then and said, "I ever tell you what a sweet-smelling woman you are?"

She laughed deep in her throat and said, "All the time."

"Well, you still are."

He tightened his arms around her, and she moaned as he bit her gently.

The knock came again. Clint pulled his nose away from her neck and his mouth away from her ear and shouted, "What?"

"Uh . . . there's a letter for you, Mr. Adams."

It was the voice of the desk clerk from downstairs, and he was obviously nervous.

"Just hold it at the desk until later," Clint said loudly.

"I thought you might, uh, want it—it might be important—"

"I said hold it at the desk," Clint shouted again. "I'll pick it up later."

"Uh . . . all right, sir," the clerk replied. "I'll, uh, hold it down at the desk."

"Good thought," Clint murmured with his mouth against Lisa's shoulder.

"It might be important," she whispered as he started to nibble her again. She wasn't only sweet-smelling, she was also *tasty*.

He licked her shoulder and slid his hand down between her legs, where he found her hot and wet.

"So is this."

He rolled atop her and slid his hard penis into her. She caught her breath.

"Oooh . . . yessss . . ." she agreed.

TWO

When Clint went downstairs for breakfast he picked up the letter from the front desk.

"I'm, uh, sorry if I disturbed you, Mr. Adams," the clerk stammered.

"That's all right," Clint said. "No problem. If anyone wants me, I'll be in the dining room."

Clint remembered the first time he had come to Labyrinth, Texas. The hotel had been smaller and did not have a dining room. That was what, eight or ten years ago? During that time Labyrinth had grown by leaps and bounds. The hotel was now two stories high and not only had its own dining room, but a saloon, as well. Also, there was a second hotel in town. Soon, he thought, the town might be too big for him to hide in, and he'd have to find another place to stay when all he wanted was to be left alone.

He went into the dining room and told the waiter, Eric, that he'd be dining alone. Like most saloon girls, Lisa was not a breakfast person.

"The usual, sir?"

"Yeah, Eric, I'll have the usual," Clint said, which meant steak and eggs and lots of hot, black coffee.

Sometimes Clint went over to Rick's Place to have breakfast with Rick, but there were just as many times when he had the meal alone. Breakfast was actually his favorite meal, because he thought of it as the most quiet. This was, in fact, his quiet time, and he valued it. Among other things, he often used the time to read his mail. Today that consisted of one letter, with no return address.

Clint had opened many letters in his time that were calls for help from one friend or another. He examined the cramped handwriting on the front of the envelope. It looked as if someone had scrawled the address hastily just prior to mailing it. He had a bad feeling as he slid a thumb beneath the flap of the envelope and opened it.

As he suspected, it was from a friend, and it *was* a request for his presence.

The letter was from Jane Cannary, known to most as "Calamity Jane." Clint knew Jane through his friend Wild Bill Hickok, but he hadn't seen her or heard from her since Bill had been killed in Deadwood, so not only was it a surprise to hear from her, but also to find that she wanted him to meet her in Deadwood.

Clint refolded the letter, replaced it in the envelope, and set it on the other side of the table. He left it there through his first pot of coffee, all the way through breakfast, and most of the way into a second pot of coffee. He never forgot about it, and in fact kept his eyes on it most of the time. Anyone looking on might think that he was leaving it there for someone to read, perhaps someone who would be joining him. No one was joining him, though. He simply did not want to think about it until he was finished with his breakfast. He stared at it, ate his food, and did not think about the contents.

Finally, after Eric had cleared away the debris of breakfast, Clint poured the next to last cup of coffee from the second pot, then reached over, picked up the envelope, took the letter out, and read it again.

It was short and to the point:

Dear Clint,

   Please meet me in Deadwood. Need your help. I know this is a lot to ask, but I need your help.

                              Jane Cannary

She knew it was a lot to ask because she knew that Clint had not been back to Deadwood since he had gone there shortly after Bill's death.

The first thing Clint had done upon hearing of Bill Hickok's death at the hands of the back-shooter, Jack McCall, was crawl into a bottle. It was Rick Hartman who pulled him out of that bottle. Following that, Clint had gone to Deadwood. He had not been back since.

Clint thought about Hickok often. He had been a good friend, the best hand with a gun Clint had ever known. He had been shot in the back by McCall while playing poker in a Deadwood saloon. It was possibly the only time in Clint's memory that he knew of Hickok *not* sitting facing the door.

Hickok's death had also caused Clint to think about his own mortality. He had always felt—and still did—that he would come to his end by virtue of a bullet, but what he didn't want to happen was for that bullet to take him in the back.

He didn't think about it as much as he used to, but Jane's letter was bringing it all back.

He really didn't know Calamity Jane all that well. He knew that she'd been involved with Hickok, that she *loved* Hickok. He didn't know for a fact that Bill loved her, but then he didn't know for a fact that his friend *hadn't* loved her.

Now she was asking him to meet her in Deadwood. What the hell was *she* doing in Deadwood, where the man she loved had been killed? If anything struck Clint as odd, it was the thought of Calamity Jane *and* Clint Adams being in Deadwood at the same time.

Was he going to go?

He didn't know yet.

THREE

"Are you going to go?" Rick Hartman asked.

"Don't know yet," Clint said.

He'd thought about it all day, and it was only now, in the early evening, that he had come to Rick's Place to talk to Rick Hartman about it.

Hartman remembered the time Hickok had been killed and what it had done to Clint Adams. He wasn't at all sure that his friend should go back to Deadwood after all this time had passed.

"I think you should forget it."

"And what about Jane?"

Hartman shrugged.

"Write her a letter," he said, "tell her you can't make it."

"Why?"

"Why do you have to tell her why?" Hartman asked. "Just tell her you can't come."

Clint shook his head.

"I can't do that."

"Sure you can," Hartman said, "you just won't. Do you know why?"

"Why?"

"Because she asked you for your help."

They had gone through this many times before.

"You've never said no to anyone who asked you for your help," Hartman said. "Don't you think it's time you started?"

"I don't know," Clint said. "Maybe I should wait until *you* ask me for help."

"That's different."

"Why is it different?"

"Because we're friends," Hartman said. "You admitted yourself that you don't know Jane Cannary that well."

"She was Bill's friend."

"Okay," Hartman said, "she was Bill's friend and you were Bill's friend. What does that mean, that you have to come running whenever she calls?"

"I'm not going to go running," Clint said, making wet circles on the top of the table with the bottom of his beer mug and then studying them carefully. "I'm just going to ride over there and see what she needs."

"Well, there!" Hartman said.

"What?" Clint asked, looking at him.

"You've made up your mind already, haven't you?"

Clint studied his friend for a moment, then said, "Yeah, I guess I have."

"There you go."

Clint finished his beer and put the empty mug down carefully in one of the already existing circles.

"I'd better get packed and outfitted," he said, standing up. "I'll leave in the morning."

"That's one thing I've always admired about you, Clint," Hartman said.

"What's that?"

"When you make up your mind to do something, by God, you do it."

Clint shrugged.

"It's the only way I know how to do it."

"I know," Hartman said. "Be back later for a drink?"

"If you're buying."

"Sure," Hartman said, nodding his head, "I'll buy."

"Then I'll be back."

Clint started for the door, pausing only to wave at Lisa Wilkes, who was standing at the bar waiting for some drinks.

Hartman watched his friend walk out through the batwing doors and hoped that he knew what he was doing. He also knew that acting immediately was just one of the many things he admired about the man most people knew only as the Gunsmith.

He was glad that he knew him a lot better than that.

By the time Lisa showed up at his door that night, he had everything ready for his trip to

Deadwood. He waited until after they had made love and were lying side by side, regaining their breath, before he told her he was leaving town for a while.

"When?" she asked.

"Tomorrow, early."

"I see."

"I have to go and help a friend."

"When will you be back?"

"I don't know, Lisa."

"I might not be here when you do come back," she said carefully.

"I know."

"What do you think of that?"

He shrugged.

"I can't tell you when to go and when to stay."

She sighed and said, "No, I guess you can't."

He waited then to see if she was going to attempt to turn the pleasant week they'd had into something that it wasn't. He didn't know her well enough to know if she was that kind of woman or not.

Moments later he realized that she had fallen asleep. Apparently, she wasn't that kind of woman.

FOUR

Calamity Jane was old Deadwood, the Deadwood of '76, where Wild Bill Hickok was shot in the back and "Preacher Smith" was killed by the Indians. It was Calamity who brought the Preacher back to town after he was killed, lamenting that the Indians had killed the only man who had come to Deadwood Gulch to tell them all how to live.

In '76 Martha Jane Cannary's name was constantly linked with that of Wild Bill Hickok. By her own admission Hickok was the only man she had ever loved.

When she returned to Deadwood, though, she did so as Mrs. Burke, and brought along with her a seven-year-old daughter.

It had been some years since Calamity had been in Deadwood, but she was there because she counted on her old friends remembering her.

It was her intention to send her daughter to a convent, and for that she needed help. She had contacted a man in Deadwood, a friend of hers known to all as the General, and he had arranged for the town of Deadwood to hold a benefit for her. It was to be held in another monument to '76 called the Green Front.

The years that she had been away, Deadwood had grown from the wide-open gold mining camp it had once been to a thriving, albeit small city. There were two- and three-story buildings where once there had been shacks, and at the end of Main Street was a brick schoolhouse. Homes had sprung up around the town, most notably along the slopes of the Forest Hills.

One of the first things she had done upon her arrival in Deadwood was to visit the grave site of her old friend, Wild Bill Hickok.

Hickok lay buried beneath a life-size pink stone statue of himself, and although a screen had been erected around it to protect it, the statue was still missing a piece of its nose.

"Who's that, Mommy?" her daughter had asked.

She had looked down at the little girl whose hand she was holding and said, "That was the man who might have been your daddy, if some back-shootin' coward hadn't killed him first."

After visiting the grave site, she had gone to see the General.

"Jane," the kindly old man said, "it's good to see you."

"Good to see you, too, General," she said. "Kind of brings back the old days, don't it?"

"It sure does," he said. "Please, sit down." The old man hunkered down next to the little girl, Jean, and said, "Hello, sweetheart."

"Are you my grandpa?" the little girl asked.

"How sweet," the General said. "No, dear, I'm not your grandpa, but if you like while you're here, you can call me that."

The little girl scrunched up her face while she thought that over and then said, "I think I'll call you the General. That's what my momma calls you."

"That's fine, sweetheart," the man said. He stood up and moved around behind his desk. "Everything is ready for the benefit, Jane. The doors of the Green Front will be opened for it."

"That's good, General," Calamity said. "I really appreciate this."

"You know, a lot of the old crowd are gone," the General said. "Slippery Jim, Bedrock Tom, Cold Deck Johnny, Bummer Dan—"

"Tell me who's still here," Jane said, interrupting him.

"Well, Porter's still here. You remember Porter Warner, editor of the *Times*. Then there's Bill Bonham of the *Pioneer*, Mike Russell, Captain Gardner, George Ayers—oh, and Doc Babcock. There's still enough of your old friends around."

"Well, that's good," Jane said. She'd been starting to worry that she'd made the trip for nothing.

"Rest your mind, Jane," the General said, seeing her concern, "even if many of your old friends aren't here, a lot of people have heard the stories about you and Bill in '76, and you nursing the miners through the smallpox in '78. You'll be able to send your little girl to the convent of your choice, I guarantee."

Calamity put her hand on her daughter's head, stroking the little girl's hair, which was as dark as Calamity's had once been. Calamity had led a hard life, and though she was only in her thirties, her hair was not quite as dark as it used to be. Still a striking woman, she was no longer the beauty she had once been, either. Still, it wasn't her appearance people remembered her for, but her courage and fire.

"I'm still expectin' another friend to show up in town," Jane told the General.

"Oh, and who's that?"

"Clint Adams."

"Of course," the General said, nodding, "Bill's old friend, and himself a legend."

"I wrote to him, made him think I needed him to get me out of some trouble," Jane said. "It was dishonest, I know, but I thought I might need him here."

"I don't think he'll be angry when he arrives and discovers why you called for him," the General said. "When will he be coming?"

"I don't know," she said. "I wrote to him from back East and couldn't wait for a reply."

"Well," the General said, "I hope he arrives in time for the benefit, which will be at the end of the week. Saturday night, as a matter of fact."

"I hope so, too," she said. "It'll be nice to see him again."

"Yes, well," the General said, rising, "as you've only just arrived, let's see about getting you and this adorable little girl settled in, shall we?"

FIVE

On the Monday that followed the Saturday of the benefit for Calamity Jane, Clint Adams rode into Deadwood.

It was funny, but he had none of the feelings he thought he'd have. He'd thought about it during the long ride from Texas. He imagined everything from doubt to fear to disgust, but he felt none of those things as he rode down Main Street. That was because Deadwood had changed so drastically from the mining town it had been when he was last there that he hardly recognized it. Even Saloon Number 10, where Hickok had been shot, was gone. Back then the saloons just had numbers, there were so many of them.

He rode until he found the livery stable, passing along the way two hotels that were unknown to him. Since most of the town seemed unknown to him, he wondered if any of the same people were still there.

He left Duke, his big, black gelding, in the care of the liveryman and asked, "Is the General still in Deadwood these days?"

He didn't have to explain who the General was.

"Oh, yes, sir," the man said. "Got his office down the street a ways from the Deadwood House Hotel. They call it the Muni-cipal Building."

"The Municipal Building," Clint repeated. "Thanks very much."

Well, that made his choice of a hotel easier. He walked over to the Deadwood House, registered, left his gear in his room, and then walked over to the Municipal Building to see if the General was in.

"By God," the General said as the door to his office opened, "Clint Adams." He stood up and added, "You made it, after all."

"After all?" Clint asked.

He crossed the room and shook hands with the General, who, while he had aged, still stood tall and ramrod straight.

"Calamity said she had written you, but she didn't know if you were coming or not."

"Well," Clint said, "I'm here. I assume she's here, as well?"

"You assume correctly," the General said, but he didn't look happy. When he sat back down, his body literally fell into his chair, as if he had barely enough strength left to lower it.

"What kind of trouble is she in, General?" Clint

asked. "Why'd she ask me to meet her here, of all places, in Deadwood?"

"Sit yourself down, Clint," the General said, "and I'll tell you all about why Calamity Jane returned to Deadwood."

The General explained to Clint about Calamity's daughter and about the benefit the people of Deadwood had agreed to put on for her.

"Calamity has a daughter?"

"That's right."

Clint scratched his head and said, "I have trouble picturing Calamity Jane as somebody's mother. What about the father?"

"He died."

"And did this benefit happen?" Clint asked.

"It did," the General said, "this Saturday past, and it was a great success. Calamity walked out of there with a purse full of money."

"And what happened?"

"Well," the General said, tugging on his left earlobe, "you know Calamity . . ."

"She got drunk."

"Rip-roaring drunk," the General said. "I felt sorry for her, really. She came to town dressed so plain, Mr. Adams, that some people hardly knew her. She doesn't stand as straight as she used to, looks tired all the time. Kept that little girl right there next to her . . . most of the time."

"And that night?"

"Ah, that night it was like she forgot she had a little girl," the General said. "The sad part of it is, she was almost the Calamity of old, but she was spending that money that was supposed to send her little girl off to the convent."

"So what happened?"

"Well, you know that not even Calamity's friends want to try to stop her when she's having her pleasures," the General explained.

"Seems to me somebody should have," Clint said.

"Well, somebody did—only they weren't her friends," the General said gravely.

Clint sat forward and said, "Are you telling me somebody killed her?"

"Oh no, no," the General said. "No, she's fine. That is, she's alive and not hurt. But somebody died, all right."

"Who?"

"A fella named Parsons."

"I don't know the name."

"You wouldn't," the General said. "He came along after you left. Started to get real important, too. Until Saturday night."

"Somebody killed him."

"Shot him in the chest," the General said.

"Anybody know who did it?" Clint asked. "What's it got to do with Jane?"

"That's just it," the General said, tugging at his earlobe furiously now. "There's some that say Calamity did it, that she killed him."

"What? Where is she now?"

"She's in the Deadwood jail," the General said. "They're holding her for trial."

"Jesus," Clint said, standing up, "I'd better go and see her."

"That's not all, Clint."

"There's more?"

The General nodded.

"The money that was raised for her little girl?"

"Yeah."

"It's gone."

"She spent all of it?"

"No," the General said, "according to Calamity, there was plenty left. She claims somebody stole it."

SIX

"All of it?" Clint asked.

"Whatever she didn't spend," the General said.

"And where's the little girl now?"

"I have her," the General said. "That is, she's with my missus. It seemed like the only thing I could do, what with her mother in jail and all."

"Tell me something, General?"

"What?"

"Do you think she did it?"

The General hesitated a moment and then said, "I'd prefer to think that she didn't, but I can't say for sure, Clint."

"Did she know the man?"

"Not before she came to town this time," the General said. "They met at the benefit."

"He was at the benefit?"

"Oh, yes," the General said, "and he was quite generous, too."

"So why would Calamity kill him?"

The General simply shrugged.

"Why was she arrested?" Clint asked. "I mean, what made the sheriff think that she'd done it?"

"Witnesses saw her and Parsons together. The shooting happened late at night, so everyone heard the shots. By the time everybody made their way out to the street, they saw Calamity staggering away from the alley where the body was found."

"Staggering?"

"Drunk," the General said, "not hurt."

"Did she have a gun on her?"

"Not that I know of, no," the General said, "but the sheriff maintains that she could have thrown it away somewhere."

"Who is the sheriff?"

"His name's Ben Woodrow."

"I don't know him," Clint said. "How long has he been sheriff?"

"Not long," the General said. "Maybe ten months or so. He replaced Sheriff Timber."

"Sam Timber?" Clint asked.

The General nodded.

"I didn't even know Sam was still working, let alone sheriff of Deadwood."

"Well, he was working up until ten months ago, and then he retired and left town."

"Sam Timber," Clint said, shaking his head. "Must be close to sixty now."

"I guess."

"What's this Woodrow's background?"

"He came into town about a year before Sam left," the General said. "Worked here and there, then Sam hired him as a deputy about three months before he left."

"Was there an election after Sam left?"

"No," the General said, "the town council decided to simply appoint Woodrow to finish Sam's term. There won't be another election for, oh, about another fourteen months or so."

Clint was still standing and now he started for the door.

"I better go and talk to Calamity, and to the sheriff," he said.

"I've talked to Woodrow myself," the General said, "but he won't release her, even though I guaranteed she wouldn't leave town before the judge came."

"Is he hard-nosed?" Clint asked.

The General started to answer, then stopped and took a moment before continuing.

"I think I'll let you decide that for yourself," he finally said.

Clint nodded and said, "That might not be a bad idea, at that."

SEVEN

Along with much of the new Deadwood—new to Clint—the jail was also different. Instead of the ramshackle shack and makeshift jail cells it had been made up of when Wild Bill Hickok was there, it was now a brick building with one window and a sturdy oak door. Clint was sure that the cells would be almost beautiful.

Outside of the door, hanging on the wall, was a plaque that stated that the sheriff of Deadwood was BEN WOODROW. The wooden plaque had collected some dirt, but it was still clear that it was fairly new.

Clint decided to knock before entering, since he didn't know what kind of a man he was dealing with. He opened the door, stepped in, and saw the man at the desk look up at him. He was hatless, dark-haired, square-jawed, about thirty-five or so.

27

His shoulders were wide, and Clint judged that when he stood up he'd probably go about six foot three.

"Sheriff Woodrow?"

"That's right," the man said warily. "What can I do for you?"

"I just got into town, Sheriff," Clint said, approaching the desk, "and I thought I'd introduce myself."

"That's fine," Woodrow said, and waited.

"Clint Adams." He waited to see if the man would offer to shake hands, but he didn't.

"I see," the sheriff said. He sat back in his chair and stared up at Clint for a few moments.

"I know your reputation, Mr. Adams," he said finally. "It's been a long time since you were in Deadwood."

"Yes, it has."

"Not since Hickok was killed, is that right?"

"I wasn't here when it happened," Clint said, "but I was here right after—and you're right, not since."

"Well, then," Woodrow said, "what brings you back here now?"

"I came in response to a letter from a friend."

"And what friend would that be?"

"Martha Jane Cannary."

Woodrow continued to study Clint now, his expression speculative.

"I wouldn't have thought she'd have had time to send a letter about her trouble."

"She didn't. I believe she sent me the letter even before she arrived here."

"Why did she need you, then?"

"I was hoping she could tell me that," Clint said, "that is, if you'll let me see her."

Woodrow thought for a moment, then said, "Why not? You ain't planing on helping her escape, are you?"

"No," Clint said, thinking to himself, not now, anyway.

EIGHT

After taking his gun from him, the sheriff walked Clint into the back where the cells were.

"I'm closing this door," he said, indicating the thick wooden door that separated the office from the cells. "Just bang on it when you want to get out."

"Thanks."

The lawman closed the door, and Clint turned and looked at the four cells. Only one was occupied, presumably by Calamity Jane. She was lying on her cot, with her back to the cell door.

"Jane?" Clint called, moving in front of her cell.

She stirred, but for a moment he thought she hadn't heard him. Then she moved again, rolled over, and looked at him.

"Clint?" she said. "Is that you?"

"It's me," he said. "What kind of a mess have you gotten yourself into this time?"

She stood up from the cot and walked to the front of the cell.

"A bad one, I reckon," she said.

She put her hands through the bars, and he took them and looked at her closely.

Martha Jane Cannary had never been what you would call a raving beauty, but she'd *had* a beauty that was born of vitality. If he had had to describe her, he would have said she was one of the most *alive* women he'd ever met.

However, the woman whose hands he was holding now did not seem to have much in the way of vitality. Her hair was lank, her shoulders slumped, her eyes darkly shadowed and lifeless. In her hands, though, he detected the strength he had always known she had.

"My daughter?"

"The General has her," Clint said. "I haven't seen her, but he tells me she's well."

"That's good," she said. She released his hands and drew hers back through the bars. "She's as well as a girl can be whose mother is in jail, charged with murder."

"Did you do it, Jane?"

"No!" she said quickly. Then she ducked her head and added, "Leastways I don't think so. I was pretty drunk."

"That's what I heard."

"I know, I know," she said, "it was foolish, but my plan worked so *well*."

"What plan was that, Jane?"

"To make enough money to get my daughter a good education."

"Doesn't seem to be working too well now, does it?" he asked.

"No, it don't."

"Tell me something, Jane," he said, "why did you write to me? Did you figure you'd do something dumb and need my help?"

"No," she said, "I thought I might need your help convincin' people to come up with some money. As it turned out, I didn't. The benefit went *real* well . . . but now I need your help for somethin' else."

"And that is?"

She stared at him and said, "Gettin' me out of here, that's what."

"I can't do that, Jane," Clint said. "You have to stay here until the judge arrives."

"I don't mean breakin' me out, Clint," Jane said. "I mean proving that I'm innocent so's I can get out of here and get back to my daughter."

"How am I supposed to do that?" he asked. "I'm not a detective, and I'm not a lawman."

"You're my friend," she said, "and I need your help. I ain't never heard of you turnin' down a friend when they asked for help."

Clint sighed. Was he doomed to forever have reputations that he couldn't escape from? *He* knew that he could never turn down a friend's plea for help, but were other people starting to know it, as well?

"All right, Jane," he said. "I've come all this

way, I might as well give it a try. What can you tell me about that night?"

"Nothin'," she said.

"I can't help you if you don't help me, Jane."

"I mean it," she said adamantly. "That's why I couldn't even defend myself against these charges. I was too damn drunk to remember anything."

"Do you remember seeing—what's his name, Parsons, that night?"

"Earlier, before I got drunk, yeah."

"Did you have an argument with him?"

"Hell, no," she said. "He put up a sizable amount of money for my daughter. Why would I argue with him, and why would I kill him?"

"I don't know," Clint said. "I guess those are just questions I'm going to have to ask somewhere else."

"Well, you can start with the sheriff."

"What about him?"

"Well, he seemed in such an all-fired hurry to pin this thing on me," she said. "He's been watchin' me like a hawk since I first got to town. I just don't think he likes me very much."

"Why not?"

"Shoot, I don't know," she said with a shrug. "Maybe because he's part of the new Deadwood and I was part of the old one."

"Maybe," Clint said, rubbing his jaw. "All right, let me see what I can find out."

"There's one other thing."

"What's that?"

"Would you keep an eye on my daughter, Clint?" she asked.

"Why—"

"I know she's with the General and all, but I'd just feel a whole lot better if I knew you was lookin' after her."

"I didn't come here to play nursemaid, Jane," he said, and then realized that it sounded a bit harsh. "I can't say I'll be looking after her, but I will look in on her from time to time."

"That's all I'm askin', then."

"All right," he said. "Now, Jane, don't do anything stupid while you're in here, like trying to escape."

"Don't worry," she said, taking two bars in her hands and holding them tightly, "I only do stupid things when I'm drunk, and that ain't likely to happen in here, is it?"

He hoped not.

NINE

Clint banged on the door and, as promised, the sheriff let him out.

"She tell you she didn't do it?" the man asked as he handed him back his gun.

"That's right."

"You believe her?"

"Yes."

"Why?"

"Because I don't think she's a killer."

"I heard some pretty wild stories about her and Hickok back in old Deadwood."

"Back in old Deadwood?" Clint repeated. "This is *still* Deadwood, isn't it? I mean, *old* Deadwood wasn't someplace else."

"Almost," the sheriff said. "This is a whole new place now, Adams, and there's not much room for anyone from the old place."

"I understand some of the *old* Deadwood citizens still live here."

"Well, they adjusted," Sheriff Woodrow said. "As we can both see, Calamity Jane did not. The dust had hardly settled on her arrival before she got herself in trouble."

"Maybe she did," Clint said, "and maybe it's trouble she doesn't deserve."

"I think she killed that man, Adams," Woodrow said, "and I'm gonna keep her locked up until a judge tells me otherwise."

"Well," Clint said, "maybe I can find something out that will make him do just that."

Clint headed for the door and Woodrow said, "Now, hold on."

Clint turned.

"What are you gonna do?"

"Nothing much," Clint said. "I'm just going to go around and ask some questions."

"You're not a lawman anymore, Adams," Woodrow said. "Maybe you were once, but that was a long, long time ago. I won't have you wandering around here bothering folks and acting like one."

"I'm just going to ask some questions, Sheriff," Clint said. "I wasn't aware that you had to have a badge on in order to do that."

"Well . . . if people start coming to me, complaining about you harassing them, I'm gonna have to put a stop to it."

"That's fine," Clint said, "you do that. Until then I'll just do some snooping around."

The sheriff opened his mouth to say something else, but Clint didn't wait. He turned on his heel, opened the door, and left. What Calamity had said seemed to be true. The sheriff seemed to have a dislike for anything that was old Deadwood.

Maybe Calamity was right. Maybe Sheriff Woodrow was just in too much of a hurry to pin this thing on her.

When Clint left the sheriff's office, he started back toward the hotel, then stopped and walked in the other direction. He didn't stop walking until he came to the cemetery, and the statue of Wild Bill Hickok.

He read from the headboard that served as a stone: "Wild Bill—J. B. Hickok. Killed by the assassin Jack McCall in Deadwood, Black Hills, August 2, 1876. Pard, we will meet again in the happy hunting ground to part no more. Good-bye—Colorado Charlie, C. H. Utter."

Clint had met Colorado Charlie when he came to Deadwood after Hickok's death. He understood that the two men had become fast friends. He liked what was written on the headboard, except for the inclusion of Jack McCall's name. Why immortalize the man who had killed Hickok? Clint would have liked it better if it had just said, "Killed by an assassin's bullet," or something like that.

He stared at the statue that had been erected, with a piece of its nose now missing, and before walking away found himself wondering why they had made the statue pink.

TEN

That night Clint had dinner at the General's house and told him what he was going to do.

Before dinner he met Jane's little girl, a wide-eyed waif wearing a pink dress and a pink ribbon in her hair who clung to the General's wife's leg the whole time, staring up at Clint curiously.

"We're going to bed now," the General's wife said. "Say good night to the General and to your momma's friend, Jeannie."

The child thought it over for a moment, and then said, "G'night," very quickly.

"That's about all we'll get out of her tonight," the woman said. "She doesn't talk much."

"Good night, Jeannie," Clint said, and off to bed she went while Clint and the General had dinner.

"Are you a detective now?" the General asked, afterward over coffee.

"No," Clint said, "not really, but I've done this sort of thing before. All it ever really amounts to is asking the right questions until you get the right answers from somebody."

"You expect that someone will tell you that they killed Parsons?"

"I don't know what to expect," Clint said. "Maybe someone will tell me they saw something. Who knows? I sure don't, which is why I'm going to be asking all kinds of questions."

"Of who?"

"Of anyone who saw Calamity that night."

"My God, that's everyone who was at the benefit!"

"Was the whole town there?"

"No, but a good many people were," the General said, "and it will take you a good long while to talk to all of them."

"Well, I'll get started early in the morning," Clint said, "which means I'd better make an early night of it tonight. Please thank your wife for the lovely dinner, General."

The older man walked him to the front door and said, "You'll let me know if you need anything, won't you?"

"You can rely on it, General," Clint said.

"You know, a lot of the people who went to the benefit had only *heard* of Calamity. Even the ones who knew her didn't know her the way we did. We may be the only chance the gal has."

"Well, sir, I'd say that gives her a fairly good chance, wouldn't you?"

The General laughed.

"By God, son, I'd say it gives her a helluva chance!" He slapped Clint on the back heartily— a little too heartily, Clint thought, as he walked from the General's house back to the center of town.

All in all, the General's enthusiasm seemed a little too much for Clint. He wondered if the old man was hiding something behind all that camaraderie.

Walking back to the Deadwood House Hotel Clint passed a few saloons, but only one interested him. It was on the site where the old Number 10 had been, the saloon where Hickok had been killed.

He stopped in front of it and read the sign over the door: THE DEAD MAN'S HAND SALOON.

It seemed that whoever had built the saloon on that site knew what he was doing. The owner was apparently banking on the fact that people would come to the saloon that was located right on the spot where the famous Wild Bill Hickok had been killed.

The saloon, was, of course, named for the poker hand Hickok had been holding when he'd been shot. He'd had two aces, clubs and spades, and two eights, clubs and spades, and the jack of diamonds. Aces and eights had, from that day forward, been known as the "dead man's hand."

Clint debated the wisdom of going into the saloon. It would bring back sad memories, and yet he was curious as to what the inside would look like. If the owner was trying to cash in on

Hickok's reputation, how far had he gone on the inside?

Also, it was still fairly early—too early for Clint to just go back to the Deadwood House and turn in. A beer sounded good to him, and this was just as good a place as any to get it.

From the sound of things the place was fairly full. He heard the babble of many voices, and the music of a badly played piano. Through the windows he could see people moving around, and as he stood there for a full three minutes or so five men had gone in and no one had come out.

After another minute of debating with himself, he shook his head and decided to just go on inside and see what he could see.

From across the street, in the shadows, a man watched as Clint Adams entered the Dead Man's Hand Saloon. The man had followed Clint there all the way from the General's house. Actually, the man had been following Clint since he'd left the General's office earlier that day. He'd been told who the man was—Clint Adams, the Gunsmith—and had been instructed to follow along and be careful that he wasn't seen. So far he thought he had done a pretty good job.

He was wrong.

ELEVEN

As Clint entered the Dead Man's Hand Saloon he found that it looked much like any other saloon he had ever been in. If he was expecting to see a life-size painting of Wild Bill Hickok behind the bar, he was destined to be disappointed. From where he stood just inside the batwing doors, he could not see anything that remotely had anything to do with Hickok. Apparently, the owner was content with just the name above the door.

There were gaming tables along the side and back walls, offering everything from faro to roulette to blackjack. There didn't seem to be a house dealt poker table, but there were a couple of games going on in one area of the room, with the tables right next to each other.

Clint walked to the bar and found a space he could fit into.

The bar was long, running the entire length of the room, and was manned by two bartenders. One was heavyset with a red, jowly face; the other younger, tall and thin and dark-haired. It was the younger one who came up to him.

"What can I get you?"

"Beer."

"Comin' up."

The man set a cold beer in front of him, and Clint put his money on the bar. He picked up the beer, turned and surveyed the room. He wondered how many times he had stood in a strange saloon and looked it over. Men drinking and gambling, women working the room, serving drinks, dodging eager hands. He noticed that all of the house dealers were male, but that there was a woman working the roulette table. She was blond and wearing a white shirt and black vest. She appeared to be in her thirties. She talked and joked with the men, smiling occasionally to reveal even, white teeth. She was not a beauty, like some of the saloon girls, but her face had more character than those of the younger women in their gaudy dresses.

He pushed away from the bar and walked over to the wheel to take a closer look.

Idly, he wondered if the man who had been following him all day was still outside.

He had first spotted the man when he left the General's office to go to the jail. He was still there when Clint came out of the jail and walked first to Hickok's grave, then to the hotel. He didn't know if the man had waited outside his hotel the whole time—he had decided to take a nap—but when he came out, there he was, standing across the street, waiting.

He had decided not to brace the man, yet. He could do that later. The man didn't seem to mean him any harm. He was apparently just keeping an eye on him. Whether it was for himself or someone else remained to be seen. The same went for whether it had something to do with Calamity Jane or not.

At the moment, he wasn't too concerned about it. Once he started asking questions tomorrow his intentions would be clear. It would be interesting to see if he still had his tail then.

Right now he was interested in the woman who was spinning the roulette wheel.

When he got closer he was able to more accurately estimate the woman's age. She was in her mid-thirties, a good ten years older than any other women working in the place, and yet it was she who held his interest—probably because she *was* older, and more experienced.

In a lot of ways.

He saw that the players at the table were using chips. He spotted a cage to the right of the entrance where the chips were sold. He'd missed it when he first came in, and that annoyed him. A few years ago he would have entered and taken the whole place in at a glance, not missing a thing. It was a difficult thing, this business of getting older.

He walked over to the cage and inquired as to the denomination of the chips available.

"Dollar and five-dollar," the man behind the cage said. Not too large, and not too small, Clint thought. He bought fifty dollars' worth of five-dollar chips and walked back to the roulette wheel.

He found a space, his chips held in one hand and his beer in the other. He watched the woman work for a while, and at one point she looked up, caught his eyes and held them. Good, she'd noticed him.

After a few turns of the wheel, she looked at him and asked, "You gonna play, or are those chips for show?"

He smiled at her and said, "I'll watch the wheel go around a few more times, thanks."

She nodded, giving him a thoughtful look this time. She continued to work, starting the wheel off in one direction, and then the little white ball in the other. She managed to watch the board, keep track of the bets, and banter with the players— all men—at the same time. Clint could see that most of the men were quite taken with her—as he himself was.

Her blond hair was shoulder-length and straight. Her eyes looked gray, but he would have liked an even closer look at them. He heard one of the men call her "Mae." Her nose was straight, her cheekbones high, her mouth almost sad when she was concentrating, but when she smiled it lit up her face and she looked anything but sad.

Her skin was pale and looked very smooth. Unlike the other girls, she wore very little in the way of makeup, but then the other girls needed it, by the very nature of their jobs, and she did not.

She was not a slender woman, but rather built full-bodied. She was buxom, about five four, and built well through the hips as well. He was willing to bet that she had marvelous legs, full and strong.

Clint was watching the wheel, and the numbers that came up, and could detect no pattern. He also watched Mae but couldn't see that she was directing the wheel in any way. Apparently, the game was an honest one.

He made his first play, a single five-dollar chip on the color red. The payoff was two to one.

A red number came up, and he was ahead five dollars. He left the chip there, and red came up again. Now he had twenty dollars on red, and he let it ride. Black came up, and he lost. He waited awhile before making his next play.

The payoff on each individual number was thirty-seven to one, but to hit one number you had to be extremely lucky. By playing black and red, with two to one odds on both, you had a chance of grinding out a profit. Poker was Clint's game, not roulette, but he was killing time and trying to get to know Mae a little better.

When he made his next play it was on red again, this time two five-dollar chips. He hit, and had twenty dollars to show for it. He let it ride, and hit again. Now he had forty dollars. He still had thirty-five dollars' worth of chips in his hand, and he put those on red with the forty dollars that was already there. Now he had seventy-five dollars riding on the color red coming up a third time in a row.

And it did.

A few of the other players noticed what he was doing and watched to see what he'd do next, now that he had one hundred and fifty dollars.

He looked at Mae, and she raised one eyebrow at him. He *loved* women who could do that! At that moment he became bound and determined to get her into bed with him that very night.

"Well?" she asked. "Will you try for four times in a row?"

He knew what she was doing. She was challenging him—*daring* him—to let the money ride. This was her job. She was a woman, and she was challenging him in front of all the other players, so that he'd let it ride and lose. Even her words were chosen carefully. Not "Do you want to?" or "Would you like to?" but "Will you?"

But he didn't think he was going to lose. He had been watching the wheel for a while now, and neither red nor black had come up four times in a row. As a matter of fact, this was the first time either color had come up three times in a row.

"Don't do it, friend," a man next to him said.

Clint ignored the man and looked at Mae.

"Why not?"

"Place your bets," Mae said, and started the wheel on its way.

TWELVE

Some of the other players were so interested in what was going to happen that they had forgotten to place their own bets. Most of them had one-dollar chips, and no one had risked as much as ten dollars on one spin of the wheel in weeks. Here was a stranger letting one hundred and fifty dollars ride.

She put the ball in the groove and started it on its way in the other direction. As the wheel slowed, the ball fell out of the groove, bounced around, and landed on a red number.

"Red . . ." she said, and didn't even call out the number.

She pushed some chips over to Clint, who now had three hundred dollars' worth.

"If you want to let that ride," she said to him, "I'll have to get it approved by my boss."

"Okay," Clint said, "let's do that."

"Mister," the man next to him said, "she *wants* you to push your luck so you lose."

Clint looked at the man for the first time and said, "Thanks for the advice."

Mae called one of the saloon girls over and said, "Get Sam please."

She looked at Clint and said, "Samuel Teacher is my boss."

"Sam *Teacher*?" Clint asked, surprised. "Does he own this place?"

"That's right," she said. "Do you know Sam?"

At that moment a man came walking over. He was tall and dark-haired, sporting a carefully trimmed mustache and wearing a three-piece suit. The vest was covered with a floral pattern, and the gold chain of a pocket watch gleamed against it.

"Clint Adams?" he asked, looking surprised.

"Hello, Sam."

"Well, I'll be damned," Teacher said, putting out his hand.

Clint shook the man's hand, trying to remember how long it had been since they'd seen one another.

"Five years?" Teacher asked.

"More like seven, I think," Clint said. "Abilene?"

"More like Tombstone."

"That's right," Clint said, "and it was *six* years ago, in Tombstone."

"When Karen came over and told me we had a high roller in the house, I knew it'd have to be a stranger in town," Teacher said. He looked at Mae and asked Clint, "What do you think of Mae?"

"She seems to know what she's doing."

"Oh, she does," Teacher said. "What's he want to play, Mae?"

"Three hundred."

"On one number?"

"On one color."

"What color?"

"Red," she said.

"Black," Clint said.

She looked at him and repeated, "Black?"

The onlookers began to mumble. They had all assumed that Clint was going to try red five times in a row. They were surprised that he was changing colors.

"What's the story?" Teacher asked Mae.

"He started on red and hit it four times in a row," she said.

Teacher looked at Clint and said, "I don't remember roulette being your game. I thought it was poker."

"It is," Clint said. "I'm just passing the time."

"Profitably, it looks like," Teacher said.

"I guess that will depend on this next turn of the wheel."

Teacher nodded, then reached down and pushed Clint's chips onto black.

"All right, Mae," he said. "Spin the damn wheel."

THIRTEEN

"How much did you start with?" Teacher asked.

"Fifty dollars."

After the final spin of the wheel, Teacher had invited Clint into his office for a drink.

"This is good brandy," Teacher said, handing him a snifter. "So tell me, what brings you back to Deadwood after all these years?"

"Calamity Jane," Clint said.

"Ah," Teacher said, nodding, "I know that she and Hickok were close, and that you and Hickok were friends. Were you and Calamity ever . . ."

"Just friends."

"Uh-huh," Teacher said. "So you're here as a friend to try and help her?"

"You could say that," Clint said. It was more complicated than that, but Clint decided not to try and explain it.

"What are *you* doing in Deadwood?" he asked
Teacher.

"I was just looking for a town to open a place in
and settled on Deadwood. It's a growing town."

"Obviously," Clint said. "How long have you
been here?"

"A few months."

"I see by the name of the place that you know
what was here before you."

"Oh, yeah," Teacher said, "Saloon Number Ten.
I know all about it."

"I'm glad you didn't go overboard on the, uh,
nostalgic quality of the location."

"I didn't want to be morbid," Teacher said with
a flip of his hand. "So tell me, what do you think
of our little Mae?"

"Little?"

"Okay, so she's not so little, and she's not so
young, but she's still the best draw I've got. There's
something about her that the men like."

"Men," Clint said, "as in you?"

"Me? Oh, I like her fine, but I don't shit where
I eat, Clint. If I start messing with the girls who
work for me—oh, wait a minute, I see. *You're*
interested?"

"I might be."

"Well, you're welcome to try her, as far as I'm
concerned," Teacher said. "Take your best shot."

"Thanks."

"But she's been rushed by every man in town,"
Teacher said. "That's a warning."

"I'll keep it in mind."

"You've got one thing in your favor, though," Teacher added.

"What's that?"

"You're the only man who's ever beaten her . . . so far."

There was a knock at the door at that moment, and when Teacher called out, the man from behind the cashier's cage came in.

"Here's your money," Teacher said.

The man started to hand it to Teacher, and the saloon owner said, "Don't give it to me, it ain't *mine*."

The man stopped short and then turned and gave it to Clint.

"Six hundred dollars," he said, looking up at Clint. He was probably about sixty, but he looked eighty and walked hunched over.

"Thank you," Clint said, accepting the money but making no move to count it.

"Don't you, uh, want to count it?" the man asked.

"Places run by Sam Teacher usually give an honest count," Clint said. He looked at Sam and asked, "Isn't that still true?"

"Yep," Teacher said, giving the little man a hard look, "it's still true . . . isn't it, Cyrus?"

"Oh, yes, sir," Cyrus said, nodding his head, "an honest count." He stared at Sam Teacher for a moment and then said, "It's all there, sir. Really!"

"I believe you, Cyrus," Teacher said. "Now go on back to your cage."

"Yes, sir."

They both waited until the little man had scurried out, then turned to look at each other.

"Like I said," Teacher went on, "you're the only man to beat her since she got here. That ought to count for something."

"I hope so." Clint held the six hundred dollars up and said, "Thanks."

"Anytime," Teacher said. "Don't go leaving town without giving me a chance to get that back now, hear?"

"I won't be leaving for a while."

"Oh, that's right," Teacher said. "You won't be leaving until you've helped Calamity . . . what? Escape?"

"Prove her innocence."

"From what I hear, that may not be very easy."

"What *do* you hear?" Clint asked. "Were you around that night?"

"The night of the benefit? Sure, I was there. I made a very generous donation, too. I believe in educating the young."

"Did you see this fellow, Parsons?"

"Sure, I saw him."

"With Calamity?"

"That I didn't see," Teacher said. "But I did see her in here later, spending money on whiskey . . . and lots of it."

"Did you try to talk her out of it?" Clint asked. "I mean, you must have known that she was spending the money that was supposed to send her daughter away to school."

Teacher spread his hands and said, "If I tried to stop people from buying whiskey with their mortgage money or from playing my games with the money that was supposed to buy their lunch, I'd be out of business."

Clint had to admit that Teacher was right. It wasn't his responsibility to wonder where the money came from that was spent—or lost—in his establishment.

"You're right, of course."

"Clint, how do you expect to get her off?" Teacher asked.

"Do you think she did it?"

"She's under arrest for doing it," Teacher said, "and I think it's going to be up to a judge and jury to decide if she's guilty or innocent."

"I need a witness," Clint said. "If I could find a witness to what actually happened, then she wouldn't even have to stand trial."

"That makes sense," Teacher said. "But where are you gonna find a witness?"

"I don't know," Clint said, standing up, "I guess I'll just have to start looking."

"What about Mae?"

"Do you think she saw something?"

"That's not what I meant," Teacher said.

"Oh."

"Besides, I don't even think she was there that night."

"Well," Clint said, "maybe I'll just concentrate on Mae tonight, and look for my witness starting tomorrow morning."

Teacher smiled, rubbed his hands together, and said, "Now that sounds like a good plan."

FOURTEEN

Clint stepped out of Teacher's office and patted the pocket where he had put the six hundred dollars just once. He couldn't remember the last time he had turned such a profit in so little time. Luck had really been on his side tonight.

He hoped that his luck would hold up where Mae was concerned. He looked over at her table and saw that someone else was now spinning the wheel, a tall, painfully thin man with a prominent Adam's apple.

Dejected, he walked to the bar. She had probably been so embarrassed at losing to him that she'd quit for the night. By making himself a healthy profit he had probably cost himself a chance to get to know the woman better.

"Beer," he told the younger bartender.

The man placed the beer mug in front of him

and asked, "Why so down, mister? Didn't you just make a bundle at roulette?"

"I guess I did," Clint said, "but that wasn't what I was after when I went over there."

"No?" the man said, frowning. "Then what were—oh, I think I know what you mean. Mae, huh?"

Clint didn't answer.

"Well, a lot of men have gone over to that table for that reason, mister, and ain't none of them walked out of here with her, yet."

"That's encouraging."

"Hey, listen—"

Just then a woman's voice, right at his elbow, said, "Get me a beer, Nate?"

The bartender looked at her and his eyes widened in surprise.

"Sure thing, Mae."

Clint turned his head and looked at her.

"Am I buying yours, or are you buying mine?" Clint asked.

"You're the big winner," she said, moving closer to the bar and standing right next to him. Their hips were almost touching.

"Right," Clint said, putting his money on the bar. "I'm buying."

"You were lucky, you know."

"I know."

"Damn lucky," she said, picking up her beer and sipping from it. For a moment she had a foam mustache that he wanted to lick, but she took care of it herself.

"I know."

"I mean, sure, you had to know when to get off red onto black," she said with a shrug, "but red could have come up just the same."

"Sure."

"Lucky."

"Right."

She cast a sidelong glance at him and said, "*Extremely* lucky."

"Well . . ." Clint said, "it wasn't all *that* lucky. . . ."

Suddenly, she lifted her beer mug and drank the whole thing down. He watched in fascination as her fine, smooth throat worked. When she put the mug down, she wiped the back of her hand across her mouth like a man and looked directly at him.

"Do you want to get out of here?"

He matched her stare and asked, "What do you have in mind?"

She grinned at him and said, "Same thing as you, I'd bet."

He smiled and said, "You'd win."

Now her smile was ironic as she said, "Well, that would be a switch."

She marched out of the saloon then, and rather than go after her, he finished his beer and then paid for the two of them.

"I think she likes you, mister," the young bartender said.

"I think you're right," Clint said. He slapped the bar top and then walked out of the saloon.

The young bartender stared after him and then said aloud, "Some fellas have all the luck."

FIFTEEN

They went to Clint's hotel room at the Deadwood House. He unlocked the door and let her walk in ahead of him. Closing it firmly behind him, he took two quick steps and caught her by the elbow. He turned her around to face him and took her into his arms. His kiss surprised and then delighted her. She closed her arms around him and thrust her tongue into his mouth. They kissed that way for a long time.

Standing there he began to undress her. He took off her vest, and her shirt, and when he had her naked to the waist he moved around behind her. He put his mouth on the nape of her neck and slid his hands around in front of her to cup her heavy breasts. He kissed her neck and her shoulders, squeezing her breasts in his hands. She pressed back against him, letting her head fall back with a moan. He slid one hand away from her breast to her neck and turned her face so that he could kiss her from behind. With his other hand he rolled her nipple with his thumb, forefinger, and middle finger.

He kissed her neck again, then started sliding his mouth down along the line of her back. He moved his hands to her hips and went down on his knees, tracing the graceful line of her back with his tongue.

He removed her belt, and then her skirt. Before removing her undergarment he helped her off with her boots, and then she kicked away the piece of white lace.

She was fully naked now, standing with her legs slightly parted. From behind he slid his hands over her firm buttocks, down the insides of her thighs, and then he reversed one hand and brought it up to cup her. Using his middle finger he teased her until she was wet, and then he inserted that finger into her. She gasped and spread her legs more widely.

He removed his finger and stroked her with the palm of his hand, enjoying her wetness, and her smell. He kissed her buttocks while he continued to stroke her and felt her legs start to quiver as he worked her toward a climax.

Suddenly, her buttocks tensed, then relaxed as she moaned out loud. He held her tightly as her legs gave, forcing her to remain standing as the waves of pleasure coursed through her. He bit her buttocks lightly, running his tongue along the cleft between them. When he was sure she could stand on her own he reversed himself, sitting on the floor and sliding between her legs.

His face was in her fragrant crotch, and he could look up at her, seeing her face between her full breasts. She looked down at him, her eyes wide.

"What are you going to—" she started, but she stopped when he cupped her buttocks, held them tight, and thrust his face into her.

He licked her avidly, squeezing her buttocks, and she cried out as his mouth and tongue moved over her, tasting her, savoring her, getting his face wet with her.

Licking her this way he could keep his eyes open and look up at her face. Her eyes were closed and she was biting her bottom lip, maybe to keep herself from screaming.

She groaned and moaned and reached down to cup his head, stroke him, rub his shoulders, and then suddenly she was crying out and beating on them and the taste of her became stronger as she became even wetter.

He pulled her down then, into his lap, and suddenly she was impaled on him while he sat on the floor. She didn't know when he had removed his trousers, and he wasn't sure himself. All he knew was that he was inside of her now. She was hot and wet and he lay down on his back as she rode him up and down, gasping and keeping her hands pressed down on his stomach for balance as her hips rose and fell . . . rose and fell . . . faster and faster until suddenly he exploded inside of her with such force that he thought he was being turned inside out. . . .

• • •

She fell on him and they lay there together on the floor for a few moments, catching their breath. He could smell her now, the scent of sex and sweat mixed together, and he knew that he was not spent yet. He put his hands on her buttocks, which were firm and slightly sticky from her perspiration and her wetness. . . .

"The bed," he said in her ear, "let's move to the bed. . . ."

She picked up her head, looked down at him, and with a satisfied smile said, "That sounds like a hell of an idea to me."

On the bed she took over.

She pushed him onto his back and lay down fully on top of him. She kissed his neck and moved up to his ear, which she invaded with her tongue. She knew just how to do it—which was rare, he had found—and he felt chills as she kept it up for a few moments before moving to the other one.

Her skin was hot on his, her breasts heavy against his chest. He felt her pubic hair rubbing against his belly as she continued to work on his ear with her mouth and tongue. His erection was pinned between them.

Suddenly, she slid down him a bit so that her pubic area was rubbing over his hard shaft. He felt her wetting him down there, but she wasn't ready for that, yet.

She still had a lot to do.

SIXTEEN

From his ears she worked her way down his neck to his chest, licking and nibbling his nipples. All the while her hands were roaming over him, just rubbing him, getting the feel of him—his belly, hips, thighs. Very lightly her right hand brushed over his thickened penis and his testicles. He groaned when she touched him there, but for the most part she ignored that area.

She moved her mouth over his abdomen, and then instead of licking him, she began to pepper him with little kisses. It was the most incredible sensation as she continued to place these kisses on his thighs. Her hands moved up and down his legs, rubbing them and then kneading them, and it seemed that she was purposely ignoring that hard, pulsating column of flesh that *he* was very much—and almost painfully—aware of.

She was good, of that there was no doubt.

"Hey—" he said, but she cut him off before he could continue, just in case he was going to protest.

"Hey, yourself," she said, taking a little nip of his flesh with her teeth, "you drove *me* crazy and made me stand up during most of it. At least I'm letting you lie down."

Well, he thought as she went back to work on him, she had that right.

He closed his eyes, surrendering himself to the sensations her lips were creating with those feather-like kisses, and then suddenly she was doing it to his penis, placing little kisses up and down his shaft. She did that for a while and then suddenly she took the head of his penis into her warm mouth and flicked at it with her tongue.

"Jesus . . ." he said, as she closed her hand around the rest of him and began to pump him. She got into a kind of rhythm, sucking him with her mouth and sliding her thumb and first two fingers up and down him. In his experience, most women took a man into their fist when they did that, working more with the palm than anything. It was interesting—and quite pleasurable—to just feel her fingertips working up and down him.

She moaned while she worked on him, obviously enjoying it herself.

"Mae . . ." he said, and with one part of his brain he realized that he hadn't even asked her for her full name—and she didn't know his name at all!

"Mae . . ."

He was trying to warn her that he was going to erupt, when abruptly she took her mouth off of him and did something to him with her hand that quelled his desire to finish.

She straddled him then, sitting astride him, pinning his penis beneath her, and ran her hands over his torso, rubbing her palms vigorously over his nipples.

He reached for her breasts, but she slapped his hands away and then came down on his mouth with hers. The kiss was—well, violent, that was the only word he could think of. Her lips were mashed against his, their teeth rubbed together at one point, and then her tongue burst forcefully past them. She slid her hands up his arms, took his hands and raised them over his head. It took him a moment to realize that she had effectively pinned his hands above his head. He knew he had the strength to bring them down if he wanted to, but he didn't do it.

The kiss went on and on, their tongues fencing avidly inside his mouth, and then hers, and then back to his again. She broke the kiss only long enough to wet him with her tongue, a long lick of his lips as if he were a peppermint stick, and then she kissed him again, even longer and wetter than before. She seemed to like her kisses wet, and he didn't mind at all. He thought she had a tongue like wet velvet. He'd thought that when she was licking his body, and he thought it now.

She started to rub the furry patch between her legs up and down his shaft, and then lowered her hips far enough so that he pierced her finally, entering her as far as he could go.

She literally gasped into his mouth and pulled her face away from him to look at him. Her eyes were glazed, her mouth puffy from the intensity of their kisses and slack now, as if she had to keep it open in order to breathe.

She lifted her hips up and then came down on him hard. A moan escaped from her, a sound of pure pleasure that increased his own ardor. He reached down and cupped her buttocks, and then she stretched out on him, her legs straight up and down with his, creating a tightness in her that was amazing. Now when she moved on him it was as if she was literally pulling on him, trying to yank his orgasm from him . . . and it didn't take long before she actually was!

He groaned aloud as he started to ejaculate into her, and she said desperately, "Louder, yell louder . . . I want you to *scream!*"

Well, he didn't scream, but he shouted loud enough for the entire hotel to hear him, and that seemed to satisfy her . . . for the moment.

SEVENTEEN

Later she said to him, "You are going to give me a chance to redeem myself, aren't you?"

He hesitated, then said, "Why do I get the feeling we're not talking about tonight?"

"We *are* talking about tonight, Clint," she said, rubbing her hand over his chest, "but before we came up here. You know what I mean."

"I do," he said, "but what I want to know is, did you come up here with me tonight just because I won?"

"Well . . . yes."

"What?"

"If you hadn't won," she said, with a smile, "I don't think I would have come up here until tomorrow night."

"Oh," he said, "well now I feel better."

"I could make you feel even better . . ." she said.

"I doubt *that*!"

"But first you have to answer my question."

"What question?"

She found an inch of flesh to grab and pinched it.

"Okay," he said quickly, "I know what the question is."

"And what's the answer?"

"I guess that depends on how long I'm in town."

"And how long will you be in town?"

"I don't know yet."

"Why are you in town?"

"To help a friend."

"Who?"

"Can I ask you something first?"

"What?"

"What's your last name?"

"Powers," she said, "my name's Mae Powers."

During their lovemaking he had told her his name was Clint.

"I'm Clint Adams."

"All right, Mr. Adams," she said, "now will you answer some questions?"

"Like what?"

"Like will I get a chance to win the saloon's money back before you leave," she said, "how long will you be in town, what friend are you trying to help, what are you helping them with—"

"That's a lot of questions."

"And," she finished, "why did that man follow us from the saloon to the hotel?"

Clint looked down at her as she looked up at him from his shoulder. "In what order would you like those answered?"

"The order I asked them in."

"All right," he said. "Poker is my game, not roulette, but since you gave me a chance—one chance—to win, I'll give you one chance to win it back. Fair?"

"Fair," she said. "Unless I don't win, then I'll want another chance."

He frowned at her and said, "We'll talk about that another time."

"Okay, then," she said, "what about this friend . . ."

"Calamity Jane."

"Calamity . . . you mean the woman they arrested for killing Mr. Parsons?"

"That's right."

"She's a friend of yours?"

"Yes."

"Are you going to try to help her . . . escape?" she asked.

Teacher had asked him the same question.

"Why does everyone think I'm going to try and break her out?" he asked. "I'm going to try to prove she didn't do it."

"How are you going to do that?"

"I don't know how I'm going to do it," Clint said, "I just know that I am . . . going to try."

She sat up in bed, so that the sheet fell away from her, revealing her full breasts. Her nipples were a dark brown and he found himself staring at them in fascination. She also had the most incredible gray eyes.

"Well," she said, "at least you're taking a realistic approach."

"Were you at the benefit, Mae?" he asked, even though Teacher had told him that she wasn't there.

"For a little while," she said, "but I really didn't have any money to give, so I left."

"Did you see Calamity Jane there?"

"Well, sure," she said, "after all, it was her benefit."

"Did you see Parsons?"

She thought a moment, then said, "Well . . . yes, I think I did."

"Did you see him with Jane?"

"No, I didn't see that."

"At the very least," he said, "I'd like to find someone who saw them together."

She snuggled back into the crook of his arm and said, "I'm not a detective, but wouldn't it be better for her if you *didn't* find somebody who saw them together?"

He thought that over for a second and then said to himself, "Son of a bitch."

EIGHTEEN

In the morning Mae surprised Clint by waking before he did. It was his experience with women who worked in saloons and gambling establishments that they usually slept late. She woke him by poking her face into his crotch and teasing him with her tongue. When he was squirming and reaching for her head, she took him fully into her mouth and sucked him relentlessly until he exploded.

"You look as beautiful at breakfast as you did last night," Clint told her.

It was a lie. She looked *more* beautiful this morning than she had last night. Or maybe there was just something about having slept with a woman that made her seem that way the next day.

"Why, thank you, sir," she said. "That's a high compliment considering I'm wearing the same clothes."

They were eating in the dining room of the Deadwood House, and she was still wearing her work clothes.

"I'll go home and change after breakfast," she said, "*and* go to bed—maybe I'll even get some sleep this time, huh?"

"Maybe," he said, grinning. "If there's a knock at your door, just don't answer it—it'll be me."

She reached out, put her hand over his, and said, "Try me."

After Mae went home, Clint found a chair, propped it against the front wall of the hotel, and sat and watched the town come awake. Every so often he thought he recognized someone from the last time he was there, but more often than not he just couldn't be sure. He finally decided to go over and talk to the General.

"Come on in, Clint," the General said as Clint entered. "Have yourself a seat."

"Thanks, General."

"Did you see Calamity yesterday?"

Clint frowned and said, "Yes, I did, General. We talked about that at dinner last night."

The General looked taken aback for a second.

"Did we?"

"Well . . . yes, we did." Clint stared at the older man a moment and then added, "Don't you remember?"

"Of course I remember," the General said good-naturedly. "I was just ribbing you. I'm not senile yet, you know."

Clint found himself wondering at that point just how old the General was. From appearances he could have been sixty, but seventy wouldn't have been out of the picture. He always remembered the General as a fine figure of a man. If he had taken extra good care of himself, he might even have been eighty!

"How's Jean, General?" Clint asked. The question was as much to test the man as for anything else.

"The little gal is fine, Clint, just fine," the General said. "You tell Calamity she's got no worries on that account."

"I'll tell her, General," Clint said. "It will put her mind at rest."

"Good, good," the older man said. "Lord knows that gal has enough to worry about. You talk to anybody else last night?"

"A couple of people, actually," Clint said. "I saw Sam Teacher. I didn't know he was in Deadwood."

"You know Teacher?"

"We've crossed paths a time or two, yeah," Clint said. "He didn't remember seeing Calamity and this fellow Parsons together at any time that night."

"Hmm," the General said, which could have meant anything. It could even have meant that he hadn't heard what Clint said.

"And then I talked to a woman named Mae Powers."

"Mae Powers?" the General said, frowning. "Don't think I know her."

"She works at the Dead Man's Hand Saloon, for Teacher," Clint said.

"Ah, well," the General said with a wry grin, "my saloon days have been over for some time, I'm afraid. After a full day here I just dodder on home to the missus these days." He leaned forward and lowered his voice to a conspiratorial whisper. "Frankly, she won't have it any other way."

"I see."

"Well," the General said, "what are your plans for the day?"

"Questions."

"Asked of who?"

Well, Clint thought, I *was* going to start with you, but now he decided not to. The General did not seem to be very sharp this morning, and Clint wondered in he was that way every morning. He made a mental note to check in with the man later in the day to see if that was the case.

"If I'm going to do it," he said, standing up, ignoring the man's last question, "I'd better get started."

"Well, just let me know if you need any help."

"I will."

"Oh, and Clint . . ."

Clint stopped at the door and turned around.

"Tell Calamity that her daughter is fine," the General said. "We wouldn't want her to worry on that account."

Clint frowned; they had gone over this before. The man obviously didn't remember.

"I'll tell her, General," he said. "I'll tell her."

NINETEEN

Clint decided to talk to the editors of the two town newspapers first. Bill Bonham of the *Pioneer*, and Porter Warner of the *Times*. Being newspapermen, both would have been at the benefit, whether they were donating to it or not. Trained observers—he hoped—one of them was bound to have noticed something.

But if either of them *had* noticed something, wouldn't he have told the sheriff? Or would the sheriff have bothered to ask—something Clint was quite sure the man hadn't done. As far as he was concerned, he had the killer under lock and key, and he seemed quite satisfied with that.

Clint came to the office of the *Deadwood Pioneer* first and stepped inside. Even before he'd opened the door he could hear the printing press going, and when he stepped inside, the racket was deafening. How, he wondered, could a man work in this kind of environment all day and retain his hearing?

The man in question was bent over the press, looking at something. Maybe the thing wasn't working right. Maybe it was supposed to be quieter?

The office itself was small, contained within the confines of one room. The press dominated the room, but against one wall was a rolltop desk that had stacks of papers on it. Apparently, the *Pioneer* was not run on a very large budget.

Clint studied the man for a moment. Short, slight, in his early fifties perhaps, with wisps of black hair plastered to his skull in a vain effort to hide the fact that he was balding. Hell, he was almost totally bald. The hair that was on top of his head now had been combed over from the right side of his head, which gave him an odd part in his hair just above his right ear. Did he really think he was fooling anyone?

Clint opened his mouth to call out, but realized that this would be hopeless. There was no way the man would hear him above the din created by the clacking press. He could either wait until the press stopped, or walk over and tap the man on the shoulder.

He decided that the press could possibly go on operating for minutes, or hours, so he walked up behind the man and tapped him on the shoulder.

"Jesus!" the man shouted, turning quickly, his eyes wide. He glared at Clint and said, "You scared the shit out of me!"

At least that was what Clint could make out by reading the man's lips.

Clint shrugged and pointed to the press. When the man frowned, Clint moved his lips, but didn't say anything. The man strained to hear the words he *wasn't* speaking, and then turned and hit a switch on the press. Suddenly, they were surrounded by silence.

"What did you say?" the man asked.

"I asked if you were Mr. Bonham?"

The man frowned.

"That's not what it looked like you said," Bonham replied. "I was trying to read your lips."

"Actually," Clint confessed, "I didn't say anything. I just moved my lips."

"Hmm," the man said, pursing his own lips in disapproval.

"Well?" Clint asked.

"Well what?"

"*Are* you Bill Bonham, the editor of the *Deadwood Pioneer?*"

"Yes, I am," Bonham said. He reached behind him and groped for a rag, which he used to smear ink all over his hand. Clint assumed that the man had been trying to *clean* his hand, but the rag was so stained itself that this was not what the man had accomplished.

He hoped the man would not offer to shake hands.

"What can I do for you?" Bonham asked.

"I'd like to ask you some questions."

"What about?"

"About the benefit that took place here Saturday night."

"The Calamity Jane thing?"

"Yes."

Now the man brightened.

"*Great* story," he said, with enthusiasm. "Legend of old Deadwood returns to new Deadwood and commits murder."

Now it was Clint's turn to frown.

"Was that your headline?"

"No," the man said sharply. "I went with something less . . . definite. 'Calamity Jane Accused of Murder.' But I'm gonna use the other when she's convicted."

"*When* she's convicted?" Clint asked. "That's a little premature, isn't it?"

"Well, maybe . . . say, wait a minute," Bonham said, squinting his eyes as if that would help him see Clint better. "Who are you?"

"My name's Clint Adams. I'm here—"

"Clint *Adams*?" Bonham asked. "The goddamn *Gunsmith*? Here in my office?"

The look of awe on the man's face annoyed Clint.

"Look—"

"Mr. Adams," the man said, his tone conciliatory, "would you agree to an interview—"

"Mr. Bonham," Clint said, "I was talking about Calamity Jane."

"Well . . . what about her?" the man asked. "Ask me anything and I'll try to help."

Sure, Clint thought, in return for an interview. Well, if he had to promise this little man an interview for his help, and then renege on the promise, he would. After all, Bonham was a newspaperman. He was used to dealing with lies—on both sides of the printing press.

TWENTY

As it turned out, Bill Bonham wasn't much help at all. He *had* been at the benefit, and he had seen both Calamity and Parsons, but he said that he never once saw them together.

"Don't you think that's odd?" Clint asked.

"What is?"

"That they were supposed to have known each other well enough for Calamity to want to kill him, and yet you never saw them together that night."

"Why's that odd?" Bonham asked. "There are a lot of people I didn't see together that night. Hell, I stayed way the hell over on the other side of the room from my wife. I bet nobody saw *us* together that night."

That struck Clint as odd, that a man wouldn't stay with his wife, but then he'd never met Bonham's wife.

•   •   •

After Clint left Bonham, he went to the office of
the *Times*. When he walked in, he noticed quite a
difference. First of all, the press wasn't running.
Secondly, the office was larger, two rooms instead
of one. The first room was apparently where the
printing was done, and the second room appeared
to be an office. There was also a man here who was
frowning at the press, but he was a young man
and Clint doubted that he was the editor, Porter
Warner.

"Hello," he said to the man standing by the
press.

"Hello," the man replied, without looking at him.
He reached into the mechanism of the press, jiggled something, then shook his head and removed
his hand. Apparently, all newspaper offices had
similar problems with their presses. Clint wondered if this was also the case in New York, Denver, and San Francisco.

"I'd like to see Mr. Warner."

Still without looking up from the press, the man
pointed to the office and said, "In there."

"Thanks."

The young man grunted and jiggled something
else in the press.

Clint went to the doorway of the office and
looked in. There was a man seated at a desk,
his back to the door. Even in a seated position
Clint could see that the man was very tall. He
had not remembered Bill Bonham from his time
in Deadwood, but he did remember Porter Warner
as a tall, bony, horse-faced man who dressed in

tweeds. Apparently, the man's taste in clothes had not changed.

"Mr. Warner?"

The man did not answer, nor did he stir. It occurred to Clint that he either hadn't heard, was asleep . . . or was dead.

"Mr. *Warner!*" he said loudly.

"Huh?" the man at the desk said, jerking his head up.

Well, he wasn't dead. Maybe he'd been dozing.

Slowly, the man turned his head and looked at Clint. He had gray hair and bushy gray eyebrows, and Clint placed his age at somewhere in his mid-fifties.

"Do you remember me, Mr. Warner?" Clint asked. "I'm Clint Adams."

Warner stared at him for a few moments—Clint was now convinced that the man had indeed been dozing at his desk—and then he smiled slowly.

"Clint Adams. By God, I do remember, sir. How could I not remember a man of such high reputation?"

Not so high, Clint wanted to say, but instead he simply approached the man with his hand out.

Warner stood—or, rather, unfolded himself. He was taller than Clint remembered, perhaps as much as six four. There was a slight stoop, perhaps, that Clint did not remember, but it did not diminish the man's height very much.

His handshake was firm and warm, as was his greeting.

"You haven't been in Deadwood in some time," the editor said. "What brings you back?"

"Calamity Jane."

"Ah," Warner said, nodding his head, "Jane's difficulty."

That was one way of putting it: difficulty.

"Yes," Clint said. "Porter, you knew Jane in the old days. Do you think she's capable of this?"

"Capable? Yes." He held up his hand to stay Clint's objection. "Do I think she did it? No."

"You were at the benefit, weren't you?"

"I was."

"Did you see them together? Parsons and Calamity, I mean."

Warner thought a moment, then said, "No, I don't think I did."

"What about after?"

"After the benefit I went home," Warner said. "I'm not as young as I used to be. Since my wife . . . died . . . I lead a rather quiet life."

Clint tried to remember the man's wife, but couldn't. It made him feel bad.

"I'm sorry," Clint said.

Warner waved a hand.

"It was a few years ago," he said. "She took sick and . . . there wasn't much that could be done."

"Porter," Clint said, changing the subject, "I can't seem to find anyone who saw them together that night. I find that odd."

"Hmm," Warner said, "I do, too. You would think, if she had some reason to kill him, they might have argued that night."

"They could have argued someplace where they weren't seen, I suppose," Clint said. "I'm just going to have to keep asking around, though.

Maybe *somebody* saw something, and they just don't remember it."

"As I understand it," Warner said, "there was a lot of liquor flowing that night. Somebody might have seen something but been too drunk to recall it."

"Well," Clint said, "maybe I can jog somebody's memory a bit." He put his hand out and shook again. "Thanks for talking to me."

"No problem," Warner said. "Just let me know if I can help at all."

"I will."

"I like Calamity," Warner said. "I'd hate to see her get railroaded."

"So would I," Clint said.

TWENTY-ONE

Now there was a concept he hadn't considered.

After he left Porter Warner's office, he thought that he should have asked the editor if he had any reason to think that Calamity Jane was actually being railroaded by someone, framed for the murder of Parsons. Initially, he had just thought that the sheriff latched onto his most likely suspect and was happy with that. Could the lawman have been involved in a plot to frame her? And if so, whose plot was it?

Clint decided maybe it was time to talk to someone who knew Calamity better than he did, maybe even better than the General did.

"Doc Babcock?"

The old medical man looked up at Clint, holding his door open with one gnarled hand. Clint looked

at the other hand, and it, too, was showing the
signs of age. He wondered how the man could
continue to practice medicine with his hands that
way. Then again, if he was the only doctor in town,
what choice would anyone have?

There was a time, in old Deadwood, when
the miners had come down with smallpox. Doc
Babcock was fighting a losing battle, and it was
Calamity who decided to stay with the miners
and tend to them, giving them as much attention
as they needed to recover. The doctor had warned
her that she could become afflicted with the dread
disease, but that didn't sway Calamity. Her position during that time had been a big reason why
she had reached legend status, at least in Deadwood.

"Clint Adams?"

"That's right, Doc," Clint said. "I was here shortly after Hickok was killed."

"Hickok," the doctor said, frowning. He looked
down for a moment, then back up at Clint. "What
do you want?"

"I want to talk to you."

"About what?"

"Calamity Jane."

That got the old man's attention. His head,
which up until now had seemed too heavy for his
scrawny neck, lifted, and his watery eyes widened.

"Jane? You want to help Jane?"

"That's right."

"Come in."

Clint had gone to the doctor's office in town, but
had found it locked. He found out that the doctor

had a house at the north end of town, and that's where they were now. The doctor opened his door wide and backed away to allow Clint to enter.

"That girl is a saint in my eyes," Babcock said, closing his door, "an absolute saint. Please, come inside and sit down."

The house smelled musty and had a distinct medicinal odor. It smelled like a doctor's house was supposed to smell.

"Do you know what she did for the miners during the smallpox epidemic?"

"Everyone knows about that, Doc," Clint said, sitting down on a beat-up old sofa.

"Well, now she's in jail and they're saying she killed a man," Babcock said. He sank into another chair across from Clint. "She *saved* dozens of lives at the risk of her own, Mr. Adams. Why would she kill Parsons?"

"They said she was drunk."

Babcock laughed without humor.

"Okay, so she got drunk every once in a while in the old days," he said. "And this past Saturday night she got drunk, but she was celebrating. I mean, she got the money she needed to educate her daughter."

"I heard that was the money she was using to drink with," Clint said, "and to buy drinks for others."

"I guess it was," Doc Babcock said. "That certainly doesn't make her a killer."

"No," Clint agreed, "it doesn't, Doc."

He asked Babcock the same questions he had asked Bonham and Warner, and got the same answers. The doctor had not seen Parsons and Calamity Jane together that night, either during the benefit or afterward.

"Are you gonna help her, Mr. Adams?" the old man asked as Clint was on his way out.

"That's what I'm trying to do, Doc."

Clint left the doctor's house and started back to his hotel. He knew that the man who had been tailing him the day before was doing it now. Maybe it was time to find out who he was and what he wanted.

Ben Hodge quickened his step when he thought he had lost Clint Adams. He was being paid to keep tabs on the man, keep an eye on him, and if he had to admit that he'd lost him, he wasn't going to get paid.

He broke into a trot, trying to reach the corner before Adams could get out of sight. As he turned the corner, Clint Adams stepped out of a doorway and Hodge almost ran directly into him.

"Let's talk," Clint said.

TWENTY-TWO

"Huh?"

The man was so surprised, that was all he could think of to say.

"I said, let's you and me talk," Clint said. "You been following me almost since I got to town. I'd like to know why."

"Mister," Ben Hodge said, "I don't know what you're talkin' about. I ain't been followin' you. Hell, I seen you around town an' all, but I ain't followin' you. Don't know what makes you think that."

"Well," Clint said, "maybe it's because every time I turn around, you're there."

Hodge shrugged.

"Goin' in the same direction, is all," he said. "No law against that."

"No," Clint said, "no, I guess there isn't."

The two men stood there and looked at each other for a few moments. Clint wasn't sure what to do. He'd half expected the man to just admit it, and now that he hadn't, what was he supposed to do? He was barely more than a boy, probably in his early twenties. Should he beat it out of him? What if the boy was just doing a job? Should he take a beating for that?

"What's your name?" Clint asked.

The younger man's eyes started to flick all about, looking everywhere but at Clint.

"You lie to me, boy, and I'll know it. Now, what's your name?"

"B-Ben," the boy said, "Ben Hodge."

"Son," Clint said, "I'm going to tell you a couple of things before we go our separate ways—and we will be going our separate ways."

"I don't know—"

"Just hush up and listen," Clint said. He put his index finger right in the boy's face, and Hodge couldn't take his eyes off of it. People walked around them, not giving them a second look. They were just a couple of fellas having a conversation.

"Number one, I don't take kindly to being followed," Clint said. "I don't like it at all. You understand that, Ben?"

"Yessir, I do, but—"

"Quiet. Number two, I don't know who you work for, but you give that message to whoever it is. If I see you following me again—or even on the same side of the street—then we aren't going to go our separate ways so easily again. Do you understand?"

Hodge nodded.

"Say it, Ben."

Hodge hesitated, then nodded again and hurriedly said, "Yessir."

"If you're just doing a job of work, then you better find yourself some other job to do," Clint said. "If you're following me because you're of a mind to try me, then let's have at it right now."

He could see by the look in the younger man's eyes that he wasn't ready to do that.

"It's your choice."

The boy swallowed and said, "Mister, if you don't mind, I'd just as soon go my own way."

"Well, that's a fine decision, son," Clint said, "a fine decision. I commend you on that."

They stared at each other a few more seconds, and then Clint said, "Well, get going!"

The boy turned, then turned again, obviously not sure which way to go.

Clint sidestepped and said, "Go on that way, and I'll go this way."

"Yessir," Hodge said, and scurried past Clint.

Clint turned and watched him. The young man never looked back.

Ben Hodge was mad, at himself and at the man who had hired him. All he was supposed to do was follow the man he knew as the Gunsmith. When Clint Adams braced him, he didn't know what to do but lie, and he seemed to have gotten away with it. He knew the Gunsmith would have shot him dead if he'd given him the slightest reason, so all he knew to do then was walk away.

It was all Ben Hodge could do not to *run*.

TWENTY-THREE

Clint followed Ben Hodge to see where the young man was going to go. He crossed the street to follow from that side, so that when Ben Hodge looked behind him—as Clint knew he'd do—he didn't see anything that would alarm him. This was the way Hodge should have followed him. Clint probably would have spotted him anyway, because he'd been followed plenty of times in his life. Still, whoever had hired the boy to do the job should have spent their money much more wisely.

Clint knew that he'd scared the boy. He hated doing that, but in this case it had been easy, and it might turn out to be useful.

The boy had obviously known who he was. That had been evident from the look that had come over his face when Clint had said that they should have at it.

The first place Ben Hodge stopped was a small saloon a few blocks from where Clint had braced him. Clint had figured that. Being scared usually leads a man to a drink first off. After that, though, Clint hoped that Hodge would lead him to the man who had hired him.

He stood across the street from the small saloon—which had no name—and as time wore on he figured Hodge was either having more than one drink or—was he that smart?—he'd gone out the back way.

"Shit," Clint said.

He crossed the street and stopped at the grimy window of the saloon. He could hardly see through the dirt-smoked glass, but he was finally able to make Hodge out. He was sitting at a three-legged table, trying to balance a beer on it. Next to him was a woman probably twice his age who was wearing a dress that would have been small on her at twice the size. Every so often the table would start to tip because of the missing leg, but one of them would catch it and they'd laugh. He wondered if maybe the boy wasn't as scared as he'd thought, but then he noticed the glasses on the floor. There were three of them, and they were whiskey glasses. They had obviously fallen from the table. One of them had broken, but the other two were whole. The boy had drunk three whiskeys, and now was drinking a beer. It wasn't that he wasn't scared; he was drunk.

That was good. He was probably trying to work up the courage to go and see the man who had hired him. After three whiskeys and a beer, if he didn't get his courage up soon, he wouldn't be able to walk. If that was the case, he'd probably end up going to an upstairs room with the woman, and then who knew how long he'd be in there. Probably wouldn't be any use to anyone until the next day.

Clint was considering going into the saloon and scaring the boy some more, but in his present state Ben Hodge might have ended up going for his gun, and then Clint would have had to kill him—and he definitely didn't want to do that.

He decided to wait the boy out and see what happened. There was a chair nearby, so he pulled it over and sat in it. When he saw the boy rise to leave, he'd step into a nearby alley and then follow him again. As drunk as Hodge was, he wouldn't have noticed if Clint followed him riding on an elephant.

Ben Hodge was very drunk. The woman sitting next to him had her tongue in his ear and her hand in his lap. She was squeezing him through his pants, and at any other time that's all Ben Hodge would have been thinking about.

"Come on, sweet boy," the woman said into his ear. "I'll bet you got you the sweetest little poke stick in your pants. Let's go upstairs and you let me have at it. Edna will do all the work."

Hodge looked at Edna. She had little pouches of fat beneath her eyes, and the valley between her breasts was all wrinkled. Jesus, if he wanted a woman he could do a lot better than this. He didn't want a woman, though, he just wanted some gumption—enough to go and talk to the man who had hired him to tail Clint Adams.

"Whatdoya say, sweet boy?"

Hodge moved his elbow, leaned on the table, and it tilted. Before either of them could catch it, the half a mug of beer that was left ended up in the woman's lap.

"Hey!" she shouted, jumping up from her seat. "What the hell is wrong with you, boy?"

"If I wanted a whore," he said, standing up, "I sure as hell would want one younger than you."

As he headed drunkenly for the door, she shouted after him, "Oh yeah? Well, there's no substitute for experience, you know!"

Clint saw the mug of beer go into the woman's lap and knew Hodge would be leaving. He left his chair and ducked into the alley next to the saloon. Ben Hodge came weaving out of the saloon, almost losing his balance and pitching headlong into the street. Somehow, though, he remained upright and started off down the street.

Clint left the alley and followed.

TWENTY-FOUR

Clint followed Ben Hodge down the street, wondering if the young man even had any idea where he was going. He was weaving all over the place, bumping into people. He slammed into a woman carrying some packages, and Clint stopped long enough to help her pick them up.

"Thank you, sir," she said. She was dark and pretty, looked like a schoolteacher, and at some other time he might have taken the opportunity to stop and make her acquaintance. This time he simply tipped his hat and continued on.

Further along Hodge knocked into two cowboys who grabbed him and looked about to kick the tar out of him when they realized how drunk he was.

"Let him go," one of them said.

"Yeah," the other said. "He'll probably fall down and hurt himself soon anyway."

They released Hodge, who almost fell right there and then. Clint breathed a sigh of relief because he had thought he was going to have to step in and save the young man's bacon.

Finally Hodge seemed to have reached his objective. He stopped in front of the building and looked up at it, as if he was still trying to work up the courage. Clint looked at the building, as well, because he recognized it. Hell, it would have been hard not to, since it was the only building in town of its kind. It was brick, and easily the tallest building in town, the one they called the Municipal Building.

Among others, the General had his office in there.

Ben Hodge tried to focus his eyes on the front door of the Municipal Building. He knew he had to go inside and up a flight of stairs. Once there he'd have to find the right office—if only his vision would clear up. He didn't mind a fuzzy head, but the blurry eyes were annoying him.

Finally, he opened the front doors and went inside.

Clint moved quickly, getting to the doors before they closed. He didn't want to go inside; he held the doors open just enough so that he could see. He watched as Hodge moved slowly to the steps and started up to the second floor. That was where the General had his office.

Clint hated what he was thinking. Why would the General hire someone to follow him? Would

it have anything to do with Calamity's problem?
Could it mean that the General had something to
do with that, too?

Well, that was jumping the gun, wasn't it? There
was no point in thinking that way until he saw for
sure what office Ben Hodge went into. If he went
into the General's, then the old man was going to
have some explaining to do.

Clint watched as Hodge carefully negotiated the
steep steps. At one point he thought that perhaps
he should go in and help the boy up the rest of
the way. As it turned out, that would have been
the wise course of action, because just two steps
from the top Ben Hodge lost his balance and fell
backward. He made a loud racket as he bounced
down the steps, and when he rolled to the bottom
he just lay there in a crumpled heap.

He lay so still that he might have been dead.
Clint hurried to the fallen boy and turned him
over. He was relieved to see that Hodge's neck
wasn't broken and he was still breathing.

"What in tarnation—" a voice said.

Clint looked up and saw the General squinting
down at them from the top of the stairs.

TWENTY-FIVE

"What happened?" the General asked.

"He's drunk," Clint said. "He fell."

"Sounded like the wrath of God out here," the old man said. "Is he dead?"

"No, but I better get somebody to help me get him to the doctor."

He stood up and looked up at the General.

"He was on his way upstairs, probably to see somebody. Could it have been you, General?"

"Well, I don't know," the General said. "Who is he, Clint?"

"I don't know," Clint said. "I don't know him. I thought you might."

"Can't see him real well from here, and I'd hate to come down there." The old man laughed and said, "Takes me too damn long to come up these stairs these days. I usually try to come up once in

101

the morning and go down once in the evening."

"Well, maybe you can stop by Doc Babcock's on the way home and see if you know who he is."

"I can do that, sure," the General said.

"I'll get him to the doctor," Clint said.

"Guess he's lucky you were here."

"Guess so."

"What were you doing here, anyway, Clint?" the General asked.

"I was coming to see you, General."

"About what?"

"That'll have to wait," Clint said. He looked down at Ben Hodge and said, "I think I can handle him myself."

He lifted Hodge up and slung him over his shoulder. The boy was skinny and light. He wouldn't have any problem carrying him as far as the doctor's office.

"Be careful you don't drop him, now," the General said good-naturedly. "Another fall on his head might just kill him."

Clint looked up and wondered if that was just an observation on the old man's part, or a case of wishful thinking.

"I'll do my very best to keep that from happening, General."

The old man was still standing at the head of the steps when Clint left the building.

TWENTY-SIX

While Clint waited for the doctor to examine Ben Hodge he lamented the fact that Hodge had not made it up the steps. If he had, Clint would know whether or not the young man had been there to see the General. Now he was left to guess until he could ask Hodge—and when he asked him there was no guarantee he was going to answer truthfully.

Still, if the boy had been going to see the General, what was it about? Did he want more money? Or was he just going to make his report? Considering that he'd had to get drunk first, it was more likely that he was going to make some sort of demand.

His thoughts were interrupted by the appearance of the doctor.

"How is he, Doc?"

"Is he a friend of yours?"

"No," Clint answered, "I just happened to be there when he fell."

"Well," Babcock said, "nothing's broken that I can see, but he has taken a nasty blow to the head. He has not awakened."

"When *will* he wake up?"

"I don't know," Babcock said, a grave look on his face. His hands, held down at his sides, were trembling. "There is a possibility that he will wake up an hour from now, or a day, or a month; there is also the possibility that he will *never* wake up."

"What?"

"I'm sorry," the doctor said, "but I can't say what's going on inside that young man's head. There may be a slight injury, or there may be a very serious one. It's not out of the question that he could die."

"From a fall down the stairs?" Clint asked. "I mean, when I saw that his neck wasn't broken—"

"The inside of the human head is uncharted territory, Mr. Adams," Babcock said. "Perhaps someone with more education than myself could give the boy more of a chance—after all, I'm just an old town doctor."

"Hey," Clint said, putting one hand on the old man's shoulder, "don't get down on yourself, Doc. You're all this town's got."

"Well, not for long."

"What's that mean?"

Babcock held his hands up in front of him and said, "Look at these. I can't even hold them steady anymore. It's not something I can hide. The town council has arranged for a new doctor. He will arrive next month, and then I'll be—well, cast aside, I expect."

"After all the years you've given this town?"

"I'm old Deadwood, Clint," Babcock said, using his first name for the first time, "and what these people want now is new Deadwood."

"Sounds like the same thing Jane is running up against," Clint said.

"No doubt," Babcock said. "How is she anyway?"

"I haven't seen her today, but she was okay yesterday," Clint said. "In fact, I think I'll go over and see her now. Will you send word to me at the Deadwood House if he wakes up?"

"Of course I will," Babcock said.

"Thanks, Doc," Clint said. "I'll be taking care of his bill."

"Don't worry about that," Babcock said. "The least of this boy's worries is paying my bill."

Clint walked over to the jail house and told Sheriff Woodrow that he wanted to see Jane.

"Suit yourself," the man said.

As Woodrow unlocked the door to the cells, Clint asked, "Has anybody been spending money around town since Jane's money was stolen?"

"Who says her money was stolen?" Woodrow asked.

"What do you say happened to it?"

"She spent it."

"All of it?"

"What else would a woman like her do with money?" Woodrow asked.

Clint decided not to debate the man. For one thing, he didn't know how much money they were talking about. That was something he'd ask Jane now.

"Just knock when you want to come out," the lawman told him.

"Thanks."

The door banged shut behind him, and he turned to face Jane's cell.

"Jane?"

There was silence, and then she said, "Is that you, Clint?"

Each of the cells had a small window, but there was a building behind the jail and not much light came in. At best, the place was always in semidarkness.

"It's me."

He moved to her cell, and she met him at the bars anxiously.

"How's Jean?"

"She's fine, Jane."

"Is she eatin' all right—"

"Jane, she's fine," Clint said. "I came here to talk to you about you."

"What do you want to talk about?"

"The money, Jane," he said. "I want to talk to you about the money."

"What about it?"

"Well, I didn't ask you this yet, but how much money are we talking about?" he asked. "I mean, how much is missing?"

"Well . . . with what was taken in at the benefit, and with what I remember spending, I'd say there was about . . . two thousand dollars left."

"Two *thousand* dollars?" Clint asked incredulously.

"That's right."

Well, he thought, if he was looking for a motive for someone to frame Jane for murder, two thousand dollars would certainly cover it.

"Where were you carrying it that night?"

"In my pocket."

"You didn't put it in the bank?"

"The bank was closed, Clint. It was late, and it was a Saturday. I didn't want to leave it in my room, so I kept it on me."

"And everyone probably knew that, too, didn't they?" he asked.

"I guess."

"Well, you were buying drinks, weren't you?" he asked. "You must have pulled the money out of your pocket more than once, didn't you?"

"I . . . suppose."

He shook his head and said, "Two thousand dollars."

"We got to get that money back, Clint," Jane said. "That money is for Jean's education."

"The first thing we've got to do," Clint said, "is prove you didn't kill anybody, Jane."

"I'd rather you get the money back," she said, lowering her eyes. "Then at least Jean will have somethin' if I—if they hang me."

Her hands were gripping the bars of the cell tightly, and he put his hands over them.

"Nobody's going to hang you, Jane," Clint said. "Not if I can help it."

She looked up at him, tears shining in her eyes, and she said, "You gonna break me out?"

"Hell no," he said.

"That's what Bill woulda done."

"He would not," Clint said, although he wasn't at all sure about that. "I'm going to prove you didn't do it and get you out of here all legal and proper."

"And if you can't do that," she asked, looking at him with cow eyes, "will you break me out?"

"We'll . . . discuss that another time," he said, patting her hands.

He wasn't sure now whether she was just trying to play him or not. The tears in her eyes could have been just for his benefit.

"You gotta get me out of here, Clint," she said, her voice firm, "you just gotta."

"I plan to, Jane," he said. "Don't worry. I plan to."

TWENTY-SEVEN

"Let me ask you something."

"What?" Jane asked.

"You know a young fellow named Ben Hodge?"

"Never heard of him," she said. "Why?"

"He's been following me ever since I got here."

She frowned.

"Why?"

"I don't know."

"Ask him."

"I can't," Clint told her.

"Why not?"

"He fell down a flight of steps and hit his head earlier today."

"He's dead?"

"No, he just hasn't woke up yet."

"Then wait until he does, and ask him."

"I intend to, but that could take . . . months."

"What's it got to do with me, anyway?"

"I don't know that it has anything to do with you, Jane, but why would someone be following me?"

"Because you're askin' questions about me?"

"Why else?" he said. "I'm not here for any other reason."

"Maybe he just wanted to try you out."

"No, I gave him that chance and he passed. I think somebody hired him to follow me."

"Who?"

He stared at her for a moment and then said, "What do you think of the General?"

"The General? Why would he hire somebody to follow you?"

"I don't know," Clint said. "I followed the boy to the Municipal Building. I wanted to find out if he was going to see the General."

"And?"

"He was so drunk that he fell down the steps."

"Ask the General about it, then, if you're curious," she suggested.

"No," he said, shaking his head, "I don't want to do that just yet."

"Well, don't worry about it, then," she said. "After all, he ain't gonna follow you no more, is he?"

"No," Clint said, "you've got a point there. He sure ain't."

"Then just concentrate on gettin' me the hell out of here."

Sheriff Woodrow hung his keys back up on a wall hook and turned to face Clint.

"Still think she's innocent?"

"Is there something that should tell me that she isn't?"

"Well," the sheriff said, leaning against his desk, "I just figure you been askin' questions all day, you should know somethin' by now."

"I know that I can't find anyone who saw the two of them together that night," Clint said. "She can't have killed him if they weren't even together."

"You forget," he said, "I arrested her comin' out of the alley where she killed him."

"Which doesn't mean she killed him."

"Yeah, well, it don't mean she didn't, either," Sheriff Woodrow said, and of course he was right.

"Why are you so all-fired sure she did it?" Clint asked.

"Because I ain't interested in making my job harder than it already is."

"In other words, you'll just take the easy way out," Clint said.

Woodrow smiled and said, "Don't make it sound so bad, Adams. Besides, she did it. You can try all you want to prove she didn't, but she did."

"No," Clint said, "she didn't."

"How do you know?"

"Because she told me."

The sheriff made a disgusted sound with his lips and said, "She was so drunk she probably did it and don't remember."

"No," Clint said, "if Calamity Jane killed a man, she'd remember, and she'd have good reason."

"Her reason don't matter," Woodrow said. "Parsons was helping this town grow. That ain't a good reason to kill him."

It occurred to Clint then that he knew nothing about Parsons. Maybe that was the way to go. Maybe, instead of looking for witnesses, he should be looking into what kind of man Parsons was, and who else might have had a reason to kill him.

Clint knew that his friend Talbot Roper, the detective from Denver, would probably be able to piece this together a lot more quickly than he could. Even his other friend, Heck Thomas, the railroad detective from Texas. But neither of them was here, and he was, and he was just going to have to do the best he could.

"What was Parsons's first name, Sheriff?"

"Dave," Woodrow said, "or David, David Parsons." He looked at Clint suspiciously and added, "Why?"

"No reason," Clint said, heading for the door, "no reason at all."

TWENTY-EIGHT

David Parsons. He knew the man's full name now, and that he was dead, but he didn't know anything else about him. That meant he had to talk to someone who lived in town, and he didn't want that to be the General, not now. Not until he could reassure himself about the man.

He tried to think of who else he could talk to. At the moment he was walking past the Dead Man's Hand Saloon. Why not, he asked himself, and went inside to talk to Sam Teacher.

He walked up to the bar and ordered a beer from the young bartender. It was early, and the older bartender was not working.

"Kind of slow, huh?" Clint asked.

"Always slow this early," the man said, giving him his beer.

113

Clint looked around and saw that none of the girls were working yet and the gaming tables were still covered up.

"Got a couple of hours before the tables open," the bartender said. "People'll start comin' in then."

"Where's Sam?"

"In his office," the man said. "You and the boss friends?"

"We know each other," Clint said. "Whether or not we're friends depends, I guess."

"On what?"

"On what the situation is," Clint said. "Mind if I knock on his door?"

"Be my guest."

"Thanks."

Clint took the mug of beer with him to the office door and knocked.

"Come ahead," Teacher's voice called out.

Clint walked in and saw Teacher behind his desk and one of the saloon girls in front of it. From behind he could see that the girl's dress was down around her waist.

"Oh, sorry," Clint said, wondering why the bartender hadn't warned him, "didn't mean to—"

"Come on in, Clint," Teacher said. "Don't worry about this. It's business. In fact, you can help me. Come over here."

Clint walked over to Teacher's desk, from where he could see the girl—all of her there was to see. She was blond and young with a pretty face that now looked worried. Her naked breasts were small but firm, with pink nipples and, from the looks of it, some bruises.

"Whatdoya see?" Teacher asked.

"A pretty girl."

The girl blushed and looked away, which surprised Clint. It also charmed him. He liked that a saloon girl still had it in her to blush—although this one *was* young. She probably hadn't been working saloons all that long.

"Okay," Teacher said, "but what else?"

"Some bruises."

"How many?"

Clint looked closer, and the girl blushed again, a rush of color that started at her neck and worked its way up. Her breasts were pale, and suddenly her nipples were becoming harder.

"Two."

"Where?"

Clint looked at Teacher.

"Go ahead, you can touch."

Clint, using his index finger, touched her just below her left nipple and just above her right one.

"Here and here," he said.

"Okay, Tracy," Teacher said to the girl, "you can fix your dress now."

The girl did as she was told, and when she was dressed Teacher spoke again.

"Can you see the bruises now?"

Her dress was cut low, but you certainly couldn't see the bruise below her left nipple. The one above her right nipple, though, just about peeked out from her dress. Just a little smudge of blue and yellow. Clint instinctively knew that the girl's livelihood for the next few days suddenly depended very heavily on him. If he told Teacher that he could see the bruise, the saloon owner would not let her work.

"No," he said, "she looks fine." Which, technically speaking, was no lie. Tracy looked *very* fine.

Teacher eyed Clint for a moment, and then looked at Tracy who was, in turn, looking at Clint. Clint smiled at her.

"Okay, Tracy," Teacher said finally, "you can work tonight."

"Thanks, Mr. Teacher."

"Don't thank me," Teacher said, "thank Mr. Adams here for lying."

"Hey—" Clint said.

"Never mind," Teacher said to him. He looked at Tracy and said, "Tell your boyfriend not to be so rough with you, or next time I won't let you work. Understand?"

"I understand, Mr. Teacher."

"All right, get out then," Teacher said. "You start work in half an hour."

Tracy tossed Clint one last grateful look and then left.

"Her boyfriend?" Clint asked.

"Yeah," Teacher said, "apparently he's got big hands and he likes to squeeze. Bad for business, though, having bruised girls on the floor."

"You couldn't see it."

"Bull."

"Not that much, anyway," Clint said, "and she is real pretty."

"I know she is," Teacher said, "that's why I hired her."

The saloon owner sat down behind his desk and asked, "What can I do for you? I see you already have a drink."

"I need to ask you some questions, Sam."

"About what?"

"About David Parsons."

Teacher made a face as if he had just bitten into a lemon.

"What about him?"

"I need to know what kind of man he was, and who might have had a reason to kill him."

"That's easy," Teacher said, giving Clint a straight-on look. "He was a low-down, conniving polecat son of a bitch, and if you're looking for people who wanted him dead, you can start with me!"

TWENTY-NINE

"You want to try that on me again?"

"Sit down, Clint," Teacher said. "Let me tell you a little bit about David Parsons."

Clint sat across from Teacher and waited.

"What do you know about him?"

"Nothing," Clint admitted. "Only that Calamity is supposed to have killed him."

"Well, if she did, I say good for her," Teacher said, "but I don't honestly think she had a motive. She didn't know him nearly long enough, if she knew him at all."

"I can't find anyone who saw them together that night," Clint said.

"Parsons was the bank manager here," Teacher said. "At least, that's what he wanted people to think."

"What do you mean?"

"I mean he didn't only manage the bank," Teacher said, "he owned it."

"Why did he want to keep that from people?"

"So that when he foreclosed on them he could do it with an apologetic smile and say, 'It's not me, it's the bank,'" Teacher said, mimicking the dead man.

"You make it sound like he *enjoyed* foreclosing on people."

"He did," Teacher said. "He was so nice about loaning money out to people to buy farms and ranches and to start new businesses, but when it came time to pay and they couldn't, he foreclosed on them faster than you could spit. Oh yeah, he liked it, all right."

"You sound like you had business dealings with him," Clint said.

"Oh, I did," Teacher said, nodding his head, "I surely did. He loaned me the money to start this business."

Clint waited, and when Teacher didn't say anything else he prompted him.

"And?"

"And when it came time to pay and I couldn't—"

"He foreclosed?"

"Worse than that," Teacher said. "He became my partner."

"Ah . . ." Clint said, seeing why Teacher hated the man.

"He didn't let anyone know, mind you, but he wanted all the advantages of being a partner—and that included his pick of the girls anytime he wanted them."

"Was he married?" Clint asked, only because he had a feeling.

"He was," Teacher said. "He was slime, Clint. Whoever killed him did me and a lot of other people a favor. I don't know how many businesses he was a silent partner in, but his partners are breathing a lot easier now."

"Well," Clint said, "you certainly answered my question, didn't you?"

"You wanted other suspects?" Teacher said, spreading his arms. "The town is full of them. All you got to do is find them."

"Why are you telling me this?" Clint asked. "I mean, that he forced himself into partnership with you?"

"I figure you're gonna keep askin' questions, Clint," Teacher said. "Sooner or later you might have come up with the information on your own. I didn't want you suspectin' me then. This way I make a clean breast of things."

Clint thought a moment, then said, "What if you did kill him, and you're telling me this to throw me off your trail?"

Teacher smiled and said, "Well, I guess you're gonna believe what you're gonna believe, Clint . . . ain't you? It's up to you."

"I guess so," Clint said, standing up. He left his half-empty mug on Teacher's desk.

"What are you going to do now?"

"Talk to the widow, I guess."

"Well," Teacher said, "that should be interesting."

"Why?"

"Because from what I told you, you probably think David Parsons was a mean son of a bitch."

"That's what it sounded like you were telling me, yeah."

Teacher smiled, shook his head, and said, "Wait until you meet Marie Parsons."

RETURN TO DEADWOOD

...through then a...d term...no...........
...er .....'s nervous now about a stage full of lead
bull but it's usually not the ...w ...'s been..............
....

THIRTY

Clint could get nothing else out of Teacher about
Marie Parsons. All he got was an enigmatic smile
and a "Just you wait."

He left Teacher's office and saw Mae getting
her table ready for the evening's games. He had
not seen her since that morning. When she saw
him walking over, she smiled and stopped what
she was doing.

"Well, you're early," she said. "Want to give me
that chance to win back Mr. Teacher's money?"

"You'll get your chance," he said, "but not this
early, I'm afraid. I've still got some things to do."

"Still trying to help your friend get out of jail?"
she asked.

"That's right."

"How are you doing so far?"

"Not so good," he said. "Mae, did you know
David Parsons?"

"Sure," she said. "He was around here a lot, almost as if he owned the place. In fact, he acted like that a lot of times."

"What about his wife?"

Mae made a face and said, "That bitch? What about her?"

"I have to go and talk to her."

"Really?" she asked. "Well, keep your hands on your belt."

"Why's that?"

"She'll have your pants off in no time, otherwise. She's a slut."

This seemed an odd thing for her to say, considering she had spent the night with him after just a few hours acquaintance—but he didn't point that out.

"She's no better than a whore."

"Why do you say that?"

"Because that's how she got what she wanted," Mae said. "I mean, I know I went to bed with you last night, just hours after we met . . ."

The woman's a mind reader, he thought.

"But she'd sleep with a man just to get what she wanted, for her or for her husband."

"Her husband used her in his business dealings? He made her sleep with men?"

"Made her?" Mae said. "No, he didn't *make* her. She liked it. She liked the power it gave her."

"Did she know that her husband slept with other women?" he asked.

"Probably," she said, "but she probably didn't care. If they both slept around, what was the difference?"

"Well," he said, "maybe he did it purely for pleasure, and she did it for pleasure *and* business."

She put her hands on her hips and looked at him with her head cocked to one side.

"If you're thinking that she killed him because he was tomcatting around, I think you're way off the mark."

"Is she attractive?"

"Oh yeah," Mae said, "she's damn beautiful."

"So why did he sleep around?"

"You ever been married?"

"No."

"Well, I have," she said. "If you'd ever been married, you wouldn't have to ask that question. Married men are always looking for something else. It's just the way they are."

"And women accept that?"

"Some women do," she said. "I didn't, but I guess Marie Parsons did."

"If she didn't kill him."

"That's right," Mae said, "if she didn't kill him."

"Did he ever, uh, try to get you into bed with him?" Clint asked.

"Oh, sure, but I turned him down, flat."

"What did he do?"

"He smiled and told me what I was missing," she said. "Being turned down didn't bother him. There were plenty of women who wouldn't turn him down."

"Why?"

"Because he was attractive," she said, "and because he had money, and he was powerful."

"Why did you turn him down?"

She smiled and said, "You should know the answer to that, Clint. I look for other things in a man."

"Lucky for me," he said.

"Are you going to go and talk to Marie now?"

"I guess so," he said, "if I can find out where she lives."

"That's not hard," she said. "I can tell you that."

"Tell me something else, first."

"What?"

"How do you know so much about Marie Parsons?"

"Because I knew her before she was Marie Parsons," Mae said. "I knew her when she and I worked in a saloon together in Wichita."

"She was a dealer?"

"Oh no," Mae said, "I worked the wheel, and she worked the floor."

"She was a saloon girl?"

Mae nodded.

"And a whore," she said. "When I showed up in Deadwood, she was already here, married to Mr. David Parsons. Naturally, that made her too good to talk to the likes of me."

Interesting.

"Well," Clint said, "maybe you'd better point me her way so I can get this over with."

"Sure," she said. "I just know that as soon as you walk into her house and get a look at her, all you're gonna want to do is get it over with."

Clint frowned on his way out of the saloon, wondering what exactly she meant by that.

THIRTY-ONE

Clint followed Mae's directions and found the Parsons house with no problem. It was a big, wood-frame, two-story house in a section of town where it was surrounded by much smaller houses. It was as if whoever had built it had decided that building it alongside the smaller houses would simply make it look larger. It was obvious that the smaller homes had been there first. They were all at least ten years older than the bigger house.

He also knew he had the right house because there was a wreath on the door. He wondered if Mae was wrong about the woman, if he'd find a grieving widow inside.

He mounted the ornate porch and knocked on the heavy oak front door. He wondered idly while he waited if David Parsons had been the man who built the house, or if he had just bought it.

When the door opened, he saw what Mae had meant about Marie Parsons being beautiful. There was much more to it than that, though. The woman's sensuality reached out and grabbed you by the throat. Even dressed in black and covered to the neck this was a woman who you could just tell would enjoy herself in bed and who would be inventive as well as responsive.

He could smell her, and he felt his body reacting to her.

"Hello," she said.

"Hello. Mrs. Parsons?"

"That's right."

She had red hair, worn to her shoulders, with bangs that reached the tops of her eyebrows. She had green eyes, pale skin, full breasts and hips.

"My name is Clint Adams, ma'am," he said. "I'd like to talk to you about your husband."

"Did you hate him, too?"

He hesitated a moment, then said, "Ma'am?"

"Well, everyone else in town hated the bastard—but you're not from town, are you?"

"No, ma'am, I'm not."

"Oh, stop calling me ma'am," she scolded him. "You don't seem at all like the kind of man who has to call a woman ma'am."

"I'm sorry, Mrs.—"

"Oh, just come in, Mr. Adams," she said. "I'll get you a drink, you tell me what you want, and then we can decide what we should call each other."

She turned before he had a chance to reply

and walked away from the door, leaving it open. Her scent trailed behind her, a mixture of perfume and . . . well, *her*.

Clint was a man who loved women. He loved them in all shapes and sizes, and all ages. He reacted to women, and never made any excuses for it.

He knew that if he went into this house with this woman, something might happen.

He went inside.

He had little other choice.

He found her waiting for him in the living room. He had taken the time to close the door and lock it behind him. By the time he reached her she had two drinks in her hands and gave him one. It was brandy.

"Thank you."

"I'm sure this is not a condolence call," she said, seating herself. "If it is, it's the first one."

"Well, I am sorry about your husband, ma—I mean, Mrs.—"

"Just call me Marie, and I'll call you Clint . . . for now. All right?"

"Well . . . all right."

"I know, you think I'm direct, and I am," she said. "It's the only way I know how to be. I'd appreciate it if you would be the same way."

"All right."

"So get on with it, Clint," she prompted. "Why did you come here?"

"To talk to you about your husband."

"What about him?"

"Well, I don't think Calamity Jane killed him," he said, "and I'm trying to prove that."

"Well, good for you."

"I beg your pardon?"

"I agree with you," she said. "I don't think she killed him, either."

He was momentarily at a loss for words.

"That stupid sheriff just picked on her because it was the easiest thing to do."

"You know that?"

"Hell, everybody knows it," she said. "I told the son of a bitch she didn't do it, but he won't listen to me, either."

"Would you tell that to a judge?"

"Sure I would, but what good would it do? I can't prove it."

"What makes you so sure she didn't do it?"

"Hell, she'd only arrived in town a few days before. There are plenty of people in this town with reasons to kill my husband."

"Marie, I—"

"And that includes me."

THIRTY-TWO

"I may be dressed in black," she said, spreading her arms, "but as you can see, I'm not exactly a grieving widow. Whoever killed him did me a favor. Now I have his money, and I don't have to put up with him."

Clint was staring at her.

"I told you," she said, with an ironic smile, "I'm direct."

"How direct?"

She frowned and asked, "What do you mean?"

"Direct enough to kill him yourself?"

"I said I wanted him dead," she said, "I didn't say I killed him."

"You haven't said that you didn't, either."

"No, that's true," she said, and stared at him.

"Well, did you?"

"If I did," she said, crossing her legs and rock-ing one back and forth, "how wise would I be to tell you?"

"All of a sudden instead of being direct," he said, "you want to play games."

"Well," she said, "I'm a woman."

"What's that mean?"

She put her drink down, stood up, and moved very close to him. She was a tall woman and her full breasts were almost touching his chest. His eyes were drawn to her mouth; her upper lip was as full and lush as the lower. Her tongue came out and slowly moved over the lower lip, moistening it. He had an erection that was pulsating so hard he was sure she could feel it, even though they weren't touching.

"Kiss me," she said.

Before he could say or do anything, she put her hand behind his neck and pulled his face to hers. Her mouth met his in a decidedly wanton kiss. She thrust her tongue into his mouth, and then covered his erection with her palm. He could feel the warmth of her hand right through his pants.

She kissed him deeply, wetly, and then abruptly broke the kiss, removed her hand, sat back down, picked up her drink, and stared up at him.

"I'm a woman," she said again, as if she had never moved from the chair, "and every once in a while women like to play games."

He opened his mouth and hoped his voice would come out on the first try.

"Did you kill him?"

She looked up at him with interest now, tilting her head to one side the way Mae had earlier while regarding him.

"You won't be put off, will you?"

"No . . ."

"Is Calamity Jane a friend of yours?"

"Yes."

"And you'd like to prove her innocence, wouldn't you?"

"Yes," he said again.

"All right," she said. "I can't help you do that, but I can tell you that I did not kill my husband, and I don't think she did. I think that if you just keep turning over rocks in town, you'll find the man who did kill him. When you do, before they hang him, I want to pin a medal on him."

She considered her words for a moment, looking off into the distance, and then looked back at him and asked, "Do you suppose they'll let me do that?"

"Lady," Clint said, "I think you're used to getting men to let you do anything you want."

That seemed to please her. But then suddenly she didn't look so pleased.

"Some men," she said.

"Most men," he said, "I imagine."

"Most men," she repeated. "Yes, I suppose that's true. Most men. There are exceptions to every rule, aren't there?"

"I suppose."

"Would you like to go to bed with me? Right now? Upstairs?"

"Yes."

"Will you?"

"No."

"Why not?"

He shrugged and said, "I guess I want to be one of those exceptions."

She studied him again and then said, "Pity. I think we'd be very good together, you and me."

"You know what, Marie?" he said. "Me, too."

And he got out of there before he changed his mind.

Outside the house he paused to catch his breath. He'd been kissed by a lot of women, but that was one of the most powerful kisses he'd ever experienced—and Marie Parsons was certainly one of the sexiest women he'd ever met. She also seemed very much in control of herself. Was she lying, he wondered, when she said she didn't kill her husband? And even if she was telling the truth, did that mean that she hadn't *hired* someone to do it for her?

Or simply *persuaded* someone?

Clint thought she could persuade a man to kill for her very easily.

THIRTY-THREE

Clint decided to go over to the bank and see if anyone there could tell him anything that would help.

The bank was fairly large, certainly more than he had ever seen in Deadwood when he was there. The town didn't even have a bank back then.

There were three teller's windows, all three presently being used to transact some business. Off to his left as he entered were a couple of desks. A man of about thirty-five sat at one, and a young woman who looked about ten years younger sat at the other. As Clint approached, the man looked up and ignored him. The woman, on the other hand, looked up and smiled. She wasn't pretty, but she had smooth skin and nice, even white teeth.

"May I help you?"

"Yes, I'd like to talk to the, uh, bank manager." He hadn't been sure what tack he was going to use when he entered, but that seemed a reasonable request.

"Oh," she said, losing her poise for a moment, "do you mean Mr. Parsons? Because if you do, uh, I'm sorry—"

"I mean whoever is the bank manager now," Clint said. "I'm aware of what happened to Mr. Parsons."

"Oh," she said. And then, "It's terrible, isn't it? That woman killing him?"

"I understood they weren't sure who killed him," he said.

"Oh, but the woman they arrested—"

"Calamity Jane?"

"Yes, that's her," she said, wrinkling her nose as if she were smelling something foul, "a terrible woman. She's been arrested."

"What do you mean, terrible?"

"Well, she's . . . uncouth."

"Are you from the East?" He looked at the nameplate on her desk. "Miss Williams?"

"Why . . . yes, I am. Why?"

"It just figures," he said. "You obviously don't know the whole story about Calamity Jane Cannary."

"And you do?"

"I do, yes," he said. "You see, she's a friend of mine."

"Oh," she said slowly, "I see." She gave him a look that said he should be more careful about the people he chose as friends. He decided that arguing with her wasn't worth it.

"Can I see the present bank manager, please?"

"That would be Mr. Cunningham," she said, sliding her chair back and getting to her feet. "Just give me a minute, please?"

"Sure."

She went to the back of the room and entered an office without knocking first. Clint waited a few moments and then the door opened and she reappeared, leaving it open behind her.

"Mr. Cunningham will see you now," she said.

"Thank you."

He slid past her, and it seemed that she was making every attempt to leave as much space between them as she could. She didn't approve of Calamity Jane, so she obviously didn't approve of anyone who would claim to be a friend of hers.

He debated whether or not to give her a quick kiss, then decided against it.

THIRTY-FOUR

Clint entered the office and saw a tall man of about forty with a bushy mustache standing behind a desk, watching him carefully. The man seemed . . . tentative, as if he wasn't sure he was supposed to be behind the desk. He was very thin, and there were remnants of something he had eaten on the front of his jacket.

"Can I help you?" he asked. "You told Nancy that you wanted to talk about, uh, Mr. Parsons?"

"I told Nancy I was a friend of Calamity Jane's," Clint said, "and that I wanted to talk to the bank manager. Would that be you?"

"Well . . . in the absence of Mr. Parsons, I have taken over that position, yes," the man said, and then added, "for as long as there is still a bank, that is."

"Is there a question about the bank staying open?" Clint asked.

"Well, I suspect that will be up to Mrs. Parsons," the man said. "How can I help you, Mr. . . . ?"

"Clint Adams," Clint said. "And you are . . . ?"

"Horace Cunningham, Mr. . . . Adams, did you say?"

"That's right."

"C-Clint Adams? The, uh, the man they call the, uh . . . Gunsmith?"

"That's right, I guess."

Suddenly, the man seemed very nervous.

"Mr. Cunningham," Clint said, "why don't you and I sit down and relax?"

"Oh, y-yes," Cunningham said, "Certainly. Uh, please, have a, uh, seat. . . ."

Cunningham sat, and Clint sat across from him.

"What do you want from me, Mr. Adams?" Cunningham asked nervously.

"Just some conversation, Mr. Cunningham," Clint said. "There's nothing to be nervous about."

"You'll forgive me," Cunningham said, "but that's easy for you to say. You do, after all, have a certain reputation."

"Horace," Clint said, "I am not going to shoot you. I didn't come here for that. Okay? I just want to talk."

"About what?"

"Not what," Clint said, "but who."

"Very well," Cunningham said, seeming a bit calmer after Clint's assurance that he would live beyond the next five minutes, "who?"

"Your former boss, David Parsons."

"What do you want to know about him?"

"What kind of man he was, for starters."

"Loathsome," Cunningham said, without hesitation.

"Then you're not surprised someone killed him?"

"I'm surprised no one killed him sooner."

"Did you kill him?"

Cunningham laughed.

"Hardly, Mr. Adams," the man said. "I am a physical coward, as Mr. Parsons so often reminded me."

"What was your position with the bank?"

"Assistant manager."

"Why would you need courage for that?"

"I didn't," Cunningham said, "which is why I was good at my job."

"Did Mr. Parsons know that you were good at your job?" Clint asked.

"He knew it," Cunningham said, "but he never acknowledged it."

"That must have been difficult."

"Yes."

"How well do you know Mrs. Parsons?"

"Not well."

"She's a beautiful woman."

"I think I see where you're going, Mr. Adams."

"Do you?"

"You're suggesting I might have killed Mr. Parsons because of Mrs. Parsons."

"Well . . ."

"Do I look like the kind of man a woman like that would be interested in?"

"Frankly?" Clint said. "No."

Cunningham rubbed his face with his hands, then put his palms down on the desk.

"I am barely able to run this bank, Mr. Adams. I was good with numbers. That was my job. I am no good at being in charge."

"What will happen if Mrs. Parsons decides to keep the bank open?"

"I'm sure she'll hire someone else to run it."

"And if she closes it?"

"That would be bad for the town."

"And you?"

Cunningham shrugged.

"There is always a need for someone who knows how to count," he said.

"I suppose there is."

"May I ask a question?"

"Sure, why not?"

"Are you of the opinion that Calamity Jane did not shoot him?"

"Yes, Mr. Cunningham," Clint said, "that is my opinion."

"And you are going to try to prove it?"

"Yes."

"I wish you luck, then."

"Why is that, Mr. Cunningham?"

"Because I don't think she killed him."

"That's interesting," Clint said. "Who *do* you think killed him?"

"I don't know," Cunningham said. "Almost anyone else in town but her."

"Parsons was not a well-liked man, eh?"

Cunningham made a face.

"There was very little about the man to like, Mr. Adams—and do you know what?"

"What?"

"He didn't particularly care."

"Which is probably," Clint said, "what got him killed."

THIRTY-FIVE

Clint stood at the bar in the Dead Man's Hand Saloon, staring into his beer. Occasionally he looked up and, with the mirror behind the bar, looked over to where Mae Powers was working.

His original plan to clear Calamity Jane was to find someone else who had reason to kill Parsons. At that time, though, he had no idea just how disliked—or hated—Parsons was. Now it seemed he had a whole town that had reasons to kill him— including the man's own wife.

Faced with a whole town of suspects, Clint found himself sorely lacking in abilities as a detective. What was he to do now? Question everyone? By that time the judge would have come to town and the trial would have been held. Then again, that might not be the worst thing that could happen.

Calamity might be found not guilty and released. Could he take that chance? Was it even up to him to make that decision?

And what if there was no way to get her released? Would he then break her out, as she had asked?

He felt tired. He turned and looked over at Mae, who was spinning her wheel. She glanced up at him and smiled, and then looked down and called out the color and the number. Apparently everyone lost, and she raked in the chips and called for more bets.

It wasn't that late; she would probably be working for another three hours or so. When she looked at him again, he made a motion, as if he were yawning. She wrinkled her nose at him and showed him the tip of her tongue for just a split second. When he thought he had gotten his message across—that he was tired and going back to his room, and that she should join him later—he turned and said good night to the younger bartender. The older one was once again working the other end of the bar.

"Want me to tell Mae anything for you?" the young man asked.

"Just tell her I'll see her later."

The bartender watched Clint leave and thought, Yup, all the luck.

Clint went up to his room, knowing full well he wasn't going to be able to stay awake. Mae would probably have to wake him to let her in, and then he wouldn't get *any* sleep at all.

He approached the door to his room and suddenly became aware of something. He didn't know what it was until he sniffed the air very deliberately. There was a familiar scent lingering there and when he realized what it was, his grin tightened. He could *smell* Marie Parsons.

THIRTY-SIX

Clint opened the door to his room and saw her sitting cross-legged in the center of the bed. She was, of course, naked. The room reeked of her scent, and he assumed that she had been waiting for a while.

"It's about time," she said. "I was about to start without you."

"I would have thought you preferred your own company to anyone else's," he said.

"Oh," she said, "you're shitty." The tone of voice she used was seductive. She had not taken offense at the remark at all.

"Why are you here, Mrs. Parsons?"

She leaned back on her hands, the position thrusting her full, round breasts forward. He found himself staring at her nipples.

"I would have thought that was obvious," she

said, eyeing him and licking her bottom lip.

Staring at her, he realized that she was not a beautiful woman, but an *arresting* one. Everything about her screamed sex—her full lips, her breasts, her smooth skin, the expression on her face, the way she had one ankle crossed over the other, giving him a tantalizing glimpse of her pubic patch.

He looked around the room and noticed that there were no clothes anywhere.

"I threw them out the window."

"What?"

She smiled and said, "I threw my clothes out the window."

"Why did you do that?"

"Because," she said, "you turned me down at my house. I did not want you to turn me down here."

"And if I do?"

She shrugged, which made her breasts do interesting things.

"I'll be crushed, and I'll have to walk through the lobby naked to get my clothes."

"You wouldn't."

She smiled at him.

"No," he said, "I take that back. You would."

"Why not?" she asked. "I have a reputation as a . . . oh, what's the phrase?"

"Slut?"

"Loose woman," she said.

"Same thing."

"Not really," she said, but she didn't attempt to explain the difference.

He realized then that the door was still open. If he closed it, it would be the same as inviting her to stay. Certain parts of his body *wanted* her to stay, but his head wanted her to go.

"Trying to make up your mind?" she asked. "Maybe I can help."

Very deliberately she spread her legs wide open, revealing the pink beneath the hair, and then put one hand there and touched herself. She closed her eyes as she drew one finger very slowly along her moist slit. He started to think she hadn't been kidding about possibly starting without him.

He licked his lips, rooted to the spot as she continued to caress herself. When a groan of pleasure escaped from her mouth, it jerked him from his . . . his . . . what? Hypnotic state?

"Mrs. Parsons—"

She opened her eyes, and they were glazed.

"I thought we were past that," she said. "Call me Marie."

"Marie . . . someone is going to come up here in a little while. . . ."

"A woman?"

He nodded.

"I see," she said, raising an eyebrow. "And you don't want her to find me?"

"That's right," Clint said.

"Well," she said, "that's easily remedied."

Abruptly, she swung her legs to the floor and stood up. For breasts so abundant they were remarkably firm. She walked toward him, and he noticed that her waist was not particularly slender, which he liked. Her thighs were as full and firm as Mae's and as she walked past him, he saw that her buttocks were tight and muscular.

And then suddenly he realized she was in the hall.

"Marie—"

She kept walking across the hall to the door on the opposite side and opened it. Then she turned and leaned against the door, one knee bent. He knew she was posing, but it was damned effective.

"We can go in here," she said. "The room isn't occupied."

Jesus, he thought.

As she went into the room ahead of him and got on the bed, he decided that Marie Parsons was not a woman to be resisted . . . twice.

THIRTY-SEVEN

Marie Parsons was totally uninhibited in bed. There was nothing that she would not try, nothing that she would not do. Clint was in that other room with her for two hours before he realized that Mae might have come up to his room by now. She might even be right across the hall at this very minute, waiting for him.

"You're thinking about your other woman," Marie said. She slid her hand down over his sweaty belly so that his penis, heavy but soft now, lay nestled in her hand.

"Yes."

"That's not very flattering."

"Not very fair to her, either."

"Who is it?" she asked. "Anyone I know?"

For a moment he considered telling her, but then he said, "No."

"Does she make you as happy as I've made you?"

"I'm not happy."

She laughed, a throaty chuckle that gave him the chills.

"Satisfied, then," she said. She was squeezing him in her hand rhythmically, and he was starting to respond. "Tell me you're not satisfied."

"I couldn't say that even if I wanted to."

"Your body does your talking for you, Clint," she said, stroking his thickening penis. "Like this afternoon, when you rejected me. I know you were like this."

She closed her hand over him, as he had grown fully hard now. She rolled over and lifted one thigh over him, rubbing her face in his chest. He felt her tongue snake out and lick one nipple, then the other. Of its own accord—or seemingly so— his hand slid down over her hip to cup her left buttock.

"Mmm," she said, moving so that the tip of his penis was poking at the wet lips of her vagina. "Oooh," she groaned as she allowed him to penetrate her just a little. "Ooh, yes. . . ."

She moved her hips so that he slid in and out of her, each time sliding a little deeper inside. He tried not to move, tried to resist, but as she took him deeper and deeper inside, his hips started to move in time with hers.

She released him then and turned so that her back was to him. She was lying on her side, and he rolled over to lie against her. She lifted one leg up and reached behind her for him. Taking hold she guided him, and he entered her from that angle, lying belly to buttocks with him behind her.

She began to move her hips back and forth again, taking him into her and holding him there, never letting him slide all the way out.

"Oh, yes . . ." she groaned. "It's been so long since I've had it like this."

"Like what?" he asked, his mouth against her damp neck. He flicked his tongue out to taste her sweat.

"So *good!*" she said.

He licked her neck avidly now, moving against her, feeling her squeeze him tightly inside of her. He licked her neck, her shoulders, her back, as she continued to moan and tug at him with her wet insides. He had no thought of Mae now, though later he would feel guilty. Now he knew only the sensations, the taste of her, the feel of her damp buttocks against him. He slid one hand down over her buttocks, along the crack between until he felt her hair, her moistness. Sliding in and out of her, he found her clit and stroked it with his finger.

She gasped and cried out, arching her back as waves of pleasure rolled over her, through her. She quickened her pace, and he moved his hips to match her, still stroking her with his finger, and then suddenly he was exploding inside of her and she clamped down on him, holding him there while he pumped out what felt like gallons and gallons. . . .

"Are you going to go across the hall to her?" she asked later.

"No."

"Why not?"

He was lying with one arm thrown across his face. She was like a mind reader. Every time he thought about Mae, Marie mentioned her—his *other* woman.

"It's better this way," he said. "Tomorrow I'll only have to explain why I wasn't in my room, not why I was with you."

"Is she entitled to an explanation?" Marie asked. "After all, you've only been here a couple days. How serious could this romance be?"

"It's not a matter of how serious," he said, "it's a matter of consideration . . . of respect."

"Ah . . ." she said, licking his shoulder, wetting it thoroughly, "respect. And do you respect me?"

"As what?" he asked.

She laughed then and said, "As a woman. As a person."

He hesitated, then said, "I don't think so."

He didn't look at her, and she was silent for a few moments—then suddenly she was on top of him, straddling him, her pussy wet on him, and he was responding, swelling again.

"You respect me for this, though, don't you?" she asked. "For what I can do to you in bed?"

He didn't answer.

"Oh yes," she said, kissing his chest, "you do." She was working her way down his body with her mouth, her tongue. "And even if you don't respect what I can do . . . you love it. . . ."

She moved between his legs, and suddenly she was licking him, cleaning her own juices off of him with her tongue and then taking him deep into her mouth. He arched his back and lifted his hips as she sucked him. He told himself there was nothing wrong with this, that she was absolutely incredible in bed and there was nothing wrong with enjoying her, even if she *was* getting her way. But then hadn't he rejected her once already? All this did was make them even.

But what about Mae?

What would he have to do to become even with her?

Marie slid one hand beneath Clint's testicles and palmed them. Her tongue worked up and down his shaft, and then she took one of his balls into her mouth, and then the other, and then licked her way back to the head of his penis before taking it fully into her mouth again. She fondled his testicles with one hand and teased his anus with the other, and as he exploded into her mouth all thoughts of being fair to *anyone* flew from his mind. . . .

THIRTY-EIGHT

He awoke the next morning with Marie Parsons curled up tightly against him. She had one hand lying on his crotch, the back of it pressed to his soft penis.

He moved her hand and slid from the bed without waking her. It had taken a long time for her to fall asleep. She seemed completely insatiable, and he wondered if she had been that way with her husband. Judging from some of the things she had said to him during the night, he guessed that she wasn't. If she had been, maybe Parsons wouldn't have been alive long enough for someone to shoot him. He might have died of a heart attack a long time ago.

He got up from the bed and pulled on his pants. He gathered up the rest of his belongings, went to the door, and opened it. He looked outside, and when he was satisfied that the hall was empty, he crossed it and entered his own room, the door to which he had left unlocked.

It was only then that he remembered that Marie had no clothes. She had thrown them out the window, and who knew what had happened to them then? Had someone found them and taken them away? Or had someone turned them in to the desk clerk?

He closed the door to his room and went to the bed to dump his shirt, boots, and gun belt. Right in the center of the bed, in a pile, were a woman's clothes. A shirt, a skirt, even a pair of boots and a frilly undergarment. They hadn't been there before, and he fully believed Marie when she said she had thrown them out the window. He had no doubt that they were Marie's, and also no doubt about who had put them there.

Mae.

Great, he thought, sitting on the bed.

Marie was right, of course. He had no real relationship with Mae. They had spent one night together. In that respect he owed Marie as much as he owed Mae—and yet he felt he owed Mae more. Maybe because he'd slept with her first? And because he hadn't been in his room when she had come to him last night?

He wondered if Mae would talk to him again, or give him a chance to explain, if he even deserved a chance to explain—and if given the chance, what could he possibly say?

He decided that a long, hot bath was in order. Maybe, if he got lucky, he'd drown.

THIRTY-NINE

Before going to take his bath, he dropped Marie's clothes off in the other room. He didn't know if it had actually been vacant, or if she had rented it. He tended to think that she'd rented it, figuring that they would use the bed in there, instead of the one in his room. She had, after all, plotted and planned to get into bed with him. That would simply have been one of her options—one that she had ended up using.

He soaked in a hot tub until the water was no longer hot, and then went to breakfast in the Deadwood House Hotel dining room. While he was eating, Sheriff Woodrow came into the dining room, located him, and approached him.

"Have you got a minute?" the lawman asked.

"Sure," Clint said. "Sit down. Coffee?"

"No," Woodrow said. Then added, "Thank you."

"What can I do for you?"

"I just thought I'd let you know that a judge will be in Deadwood in three days to preside over Calamity Jane's trial. I just got word about it."

"What judge?"

"I don't know him," Woodrow said. "Judge Robert H. Wiley."

Clint frowned, searching his memory for the name.

"I don't know him, either," he said finally.

"That means you've got three days to prove her innocence," Woodrow said.

"Well," Clint said, "thanks for the arithmetic lesson. Is that what you came here to tell me?"

Woodrow sat staring at Clint for a few moments. He seemed to have something on his mind, and Clint decided to let him get to it in his own time.

Finally, the lawman spoke.

"Look," he said, "I'm really not trying to railroad Calamity Jane into anything."

"That's good to know."

"But," he went on, "there are those in town who would like to see her found guilty of Parsons's murder."

"Just as a scapegoat?"

Woodrow didn't answer.

"Look," Clint said, laying his knife and fork aside and picking up his coffee. As far as he was concerned, his meal was over. "From the questions I've asked, I've found out that there weren't too many people in town who liked Parsons. In fact, there are quite a few who are glad that he's dead. Now, any one of them could have killed him and taken advantage of the fact that Calamity was drunk to frame her for the murder."

"But you can't prove that."

Clint started to tell the man he was right, and then thought better of it.

Woodrow waited for a reply, and when one did not come he leaned forward.

"Can you?"

"Maybe," Clint said, "and maybe not."

"What's that mean?"

"It means that I'm not prepared to tell you where I stand," Clint said. "Maybe we'll just wait the three days for the judge to arrive, and then I'll tell *him* what I've found out."

"Then you *have* found out something that will clear her in court?"

Again, Clint played his hand close to his vest.

"Maybe," he said, "and maybe not."

"Or you're just not saying, right now?"

"I need some more coffee," Clint said, looking around for his waiter. "Are you sure you don't want some?"

"Uh . . . thanks, but I've got rounds to make." The lawman stood up and very quickly left the dining room and the hotel.

Sure, Clint thought, rounds to make . . . or somebody to report to. He now felt fairly certain that someone had sent the sheriff to question him, to see what—if anything—he had found out so far. Now the lawman would go back to whoever that was and even though Clint was careful not to commit himself either way, Woodrow would probably report that he *had* found something out.

If someone was framing Calamity Jane for the murder, they had three days to act before the judge arrived. Three days in which to make sure that Clint Adams was not in possession of facts that would clear Calamity Jane.

Woodrow went right from the hotel to the office of the man he was working for.

"What did you find out?" the man asked.

"He knows something," Woodrow said, "but he's not saying what it is."

"What do you think it is?"

"I don't know," the lawman said with a shrug. "All I know is that he was looking for a witness, somebody who could *swear* that Calamity Jane didn't kill Dave Parsons. If that's what he was looking for, then maybe that's what he found."

"When is the judge due?"

"Three days."

"Then I guess we have three days to find out, don't we?"

FORTY

The minute Clint Adams left the hotel he felt as if there was a bull's-eye painted on his back. He couldn't very well complain, though. He'd painted it there himself, hadn't he? By being noncommittal with Sheriff Woodrow he had manipulated the man into thinking that he did have something that would clear Calamity Jane—and if he had something that would do that, he could very well have something that pointed to the actual guilty party.

For the next three days Clint knew he'd have to keep watching his back, or he might end up the way Wild Bill Hickok did—and there wouldn't be any statue erected in his memory.

After Woodrow left the office, the man sat behind his desk, trying to decide what to do.

Hiring Ben Hodge had obviously been a mistake. He couldn't afford to make another one. Woodrow would not be able to do the job. The man was willing to be dictated to in the running of his "office," but he would not be willing to commit murder. Nor would he be willing to go up against a man like the Gunsmith.

What the man was going to have to do was find someone who was.

FORTY-ONE

Clint went from the hotel to Doc Babcock's office to check on Bed Hodge.

"No change, I'm afraid," Babcock said. "It's too bad for the boy this had to happen out here, and not somewhere he could get proper medical treatment."

"Is there something you should be doing for him that you're not, Doc?"

"Of course not," Babcock said, bristling. But then he calmed down and added, "I'm doing all that I know how to do—but that's the problem. Another doctor—a younger, better educated doctor—might know of something more."

"Well, we don't have a younger, better educated doctor in town, Doc," Clint said. "Just you."

"Well, maybe he'll have a better chance when the new doctor comes to town," Babcock said. "He's bound to be younger and better than I am."

"Well," Clint said, putting his hand on the older man's shoulder, "younger, certainly."

For the first time since his arrival in Deadwood—the new Deadwood—he saw Doc Babcock smile.

"Please let me know if he regains consciousness," Clint said. "He has some information that will help me clear Calamity Jane."

"I'll see to it that you know as soon as he opens his eyes."

When Clint left the doctor's office, he decided to go and see the only other person in town he thought he might be able to talk to, or trust. It was funny that he would think of Sam Teacher that way. He and Teacher had literally crossed paths only a few times, but compared to the others in town, he had known the man a lot longer, and felt he had much more in common with him.

Besides, he needed a sounding board for some of the things that were going through his head.

Teacher welcomed Clint into the saloon, even though it wasn't open yet. Clint had to knock on the front doors, and when the young bartender opened them up he recognized Clint as a friend of his boss and let him in.

"Somebody to see you, boss," he said.

Instead of being in his office, Teacher was sitting at one of the tables—the only one that didn't have the chairs resting upside down on them. He had obviously just finished his breakfast and was having coffee.

"Clint," he greeted, "come in, sit down and have some coffee. If I remember right, it's a favorite drink of yours."

"You remember right," Clint said, sitting down.

"Nate, bring out another cup, and a fresh pot of coffee."

"Sure thing, boss."

"What have you been up to today?" Teacher asked him.

"I've already talked with the sheriff and the doctor," Clint said.

"How's the boy?"

"No change."

"And what'd you and the sheriff have to say to each other?"

"Not much," Clint said. "I think he was just pumping me for information."

"Wanted to know what you'd found out about Calamity and Parsons, you mean?"

"That's right."

"Well, that was easy," Teacher said. "You haven't found *anything* out."

"Well . . . that's not what I told him."

Clint paused when Nate appeared with the fresh pot of coffee and the extra cup.

When they both had full cups of fresh coffee in front of them, Teacher leaned forward and said, "What exactly did you tell him?"

"Not much, really," Clint said, "it was more what I didn't tell him."

"Did you come here to play word games with me?" Teacher asked, sitting back. "Because if you did, I have to tell you I'm not good at them."

"No, no," Clint said. "No games."

Briefly, then, he recounted his conversation with Sheriff Woodrow, and Teacher listened intently.

"You know what you've done, don't you?" Teacher asked when Clint finished.

"I know."

"You've painted a bull's-eye on your back."

The fact that Teacher said just what he'd been thinking simply proved his point. The man was the only one in town he could really talk to.

"I know that."

"I see," Teacher said, "that's what you *want* to do. You want the person who really killed Parsons—if there is such an animal—to come after you."

"I figure he'll *send* someone after me," Clint said, "but that's the general idea, yeah."

"And then you'll get *that* person and have them tell you who hired them. Something like that?"

"Something like that, yeah."

"So tell me something."

"What?"

"What if it happens the other way around?" Teacher asked. "What happens if it's *him* who gets *you*?"

FORTY-TWO

Both men looked up when they heard someone else enter the room. It was Mae Powers.

"You're here early, Mae," Teacher said.

"I just want to take a look at my wheel," she said. "I think it's a little off balance."

"Go ahead, then."

She hesitated a moment, looking at Clint, not Teacher, and then she averted her eyes and walked to her table.

"Problem with you two?" Teacher asked Clint.

"No," Clint said. "Well, maybe just a little misunderstanding."

"Don't ruin my best draw, Clint," Teacher said. "Men come from a long way off to try to beat her."

"I'm not going to do anything to her."

"You already have."

"What?"

"You beat her," he said. "She's not going to want you to leave town without giving her a chance to get back at you."

Clint knew the way Teacher meant the remark, but he was thinking of it a whole different way.

"Excuse me," he said. "I just want to talk to her for a minute."

"Sure," Teacher said, "but watch your back, huh? This town is already on the map for *that* kind of thing—you know what I mean?"

He meant Hickok.

"Yeah, Sam," Clint said, "I know. Thanks."

Clint left Teacher's table and walked over to where Mae was inspecting her wheel.

"You don't only run it, you can take it apart and put it back together, huh?"

"It's how I make my living," she said, without looking at him, "so I make sure I know how it works."

"Well . . . that's good."

"I'm a little busy, Clint," she said, straightening and looking at him. "You want to make small talk, or what?"

"No," he said, "I wanted to talk to you about last night."

"We didn't see each other last night," she said.

"I know, but—"

"Why?" she asked. "Were we supposed to?"

"Mae—"

"Actually," she went on, "I was pretty tired last

night. So when I finished up here, I went home to bed."

"Mae—"

"I'm sorry if you were expecting me," she said. "I didn't mean to disappoint you."

He started to say her name again, but then stopped. Obviously, this was the way she wanted to play it.

"Well . . . I guess that's that, then."

"Yes," she said, "I guess it is. I have to get back to this wheel now."

"Sure," he said, "sure, you get back to work."

He turned and started to walk away.

"Hey."

He turned and looked at her.

"Don't forget, you owe me a chance to get my money back."

"You'll get the chance," he said. "I promise."

"Tonight would be nice."

He stared at her and then nodded his head.

"Tonight it is, then."

"I'm looking forward to it."

He felt sure that she was.

He waved at Teacher, and the bartender let him out the front door.

Outside he felt a wave of sadness. He had hurt Mae without meaning to. If she had given him a chance, maybe he could have explained it.

Maybe.

He decided to let her have it her way, though. Perhaps this way she retained her dignity. He'd never meant to take it away from her, but then he'd never made any promises. After all, they'd only known each other a short time and only been together once.

Why was he doing this? Why was he trying to justify his actions?

Because he felt like a heel, that's why, and there was no amount of justification that was going to change that.

FORTY-THREE

The three men stood in front of the man's desk, waiting.

"I'll be paying you all a lot of money," he said. He'd been told their names, but he'd forgotten them at the moment.

"Sure," one of them said. "That is, if we live to collect it."

The man had felt it necessary to tell them just who they were being hired to kill. They had to know who they were going up against so that they would approach the job with the right attitude.

This, however, was not quite the attitude he had in mind.

"Whether or not you live to collect it will be entirely up to you," he said to them.

"We could use more men."

"You could," the man said, "but then you'd have to pay them with your own money. I'm hiring the three of you because you are all supposed to know how to use a gun."

"We do," the spokesman said.

"We're all real good hands with a gun," the second man said.

"But, uh, not as good as the Gunsmith," the third man said.

"Well," the spokesman said, "maybe not alone, but the three of us together . . ."

"*That's* the attitude I want," the man who was hiring them said. "Put your guns together—and your heads—and come up with a plan."

"When do you want this done?"

"This is Wednesday," the man said. "I'd prefer that he not see Friday."

"Why wait?" the second man said. "Let's get it done."

"Good thinking," their employer said.

"Do you care how it looks?" the spokesman asked.

"Mister," the man said, because he still couldn't recall their names, "all I care about is that Clint Adams is dead come Friday."

"All right, then," the spokesman said.

"Can we, uh, get some money ahead of time?" the second man asked.

The man behind the desk gave him a cold look.

"Never mind," the spokesman said, putting his hand on the second man's chest. "We'll collect when the job's done."

They walked to the door and then it was the first

man, the spokesman, who had a question about the money.

"Let's say one of us gets killed," he said to the man behind the desk. "What happens to his money?"

"The other two split it," the man said. "I'm paying one sum of money for the job. Who gets it is entirely up to you."

After the three men left, the man behind the desk sat back in his chair and rubbed his hands over his face. He'd just hired three men to commit murder. Not only that, but to kill a man he knew.

How had he gotten himself into this, anyway?

Bad judgment, he guessed. Bad investments. Calamity Jane's benefit seemed his chance to get his hands on some decent money—money that might help him recoup some losses. As it turned out, there wasn't as much money as he'd thought, but he'd only found that out after the deed had been done.

That murder he had committed himself, as if to prove to himself that he could. Besides, he hadn't wanted anyone else to have the pleasure of killing David Parsons. That was a pleasure he'd been looking forward to for a long time. But it was only after Parsons was dead that he'd realized how *much* he'd wanted it.

He felt badly about Calamity, but she had ridden into a situation, presenting herself as just the right scapegoat. It was not something he could afford *not* to take advantage of.

First Calamity, and now Clint Adams. People he knew, but people who had become entangled in something they knew nothing about.

It was too bad, but it was necessary.

He wiped his watery eyes with a handkerchief—they seemed to always be watery these days—and wondered who he was trying to convince.

FORTY-FOUR

Ben Hodge died that day.

Clint was at his hotel, sitting out front on a chair, when a small boy came running over to him.

"Doc sent me to fetch ya," the boy said.

"Thanks, son."

"He said you'd gimme two bits," the dirty-faced boy said.

"Well, if he said so, I wouldn't want to make a liar out of him, would I?"

"No, sir."

Clint tossed a quarter in the air and it disappeared into a grimy palm.

"Thanks, mister."

Clint walked over to the doctor's office and knew what was wrong as soon as he entered. He could tell by the look on the old man's face.

"He's gone," Doc said.

"I'm sorry, Doc."

"He never opened his eyes again." The physician shook his head. "From a stupid tumble down a flight of stairs. What a waste."

"I know," Clint said, touching the man's shoulder. "You did all you could, Doc. There was nothing more you could have done."

"He was so young," Babcock said. "I'm sorry for Jane, too. You said he knew something that could help her."

"So I did," Clint said, an idea forming in his mind.

"Now he'll never be able to tell you."

"That's true," Clint said, tightening his grip on the other man's shoulder, "but only you and I know that, right, Doc?"

The man's hands might have been shaking, but there was nothing wrong with his mind. He caught onto Clint's meaning immediately.

"That's true."

"Just remember," Clint said. "You never went in with me, you didn't hear anything. He died while I was inside with him. Okay?"

"I could back up your story—"

"No, Doc," Clint said. "It's better this way. You didn't hear a thing. Do you understand?"

"Yes, yes, I understand."

"That's the way it's got to be, Doc."

"Your life will be in danger."

"I'll have to take my chances," Clint said. "Besides, I can't have you getting killed. I may need you later myself."

FORTY-FIVE

Before leaving the doctor's office, he had Babcock tell him the name of the boy he'd sent to fetch him. He found the boy—Billy Collins—and told him to spread the word that Ben Hodge had woken up and talked with Clint Adams. He gave the boy a dollar and said he'd get another one when the job was done.

By midday the word spread throughout the town that Hodge had talked to Clint Adams, and that Clint probably knew now who had hired him.

The man sat behind his desk, waiting impatiently. This time, instead of calling for all three gunmen, he called for one, the spokesman. When there was a knock at the door, he called out, "Come!"

The spokesman of the three gunmen, Matt Doyle, entered and approached the desk.

"What's so important that I had to come back?" he asked.

"Have you heard the word going around town?"

"About Adams? Yeah, I heard. He's supposed to have talked to some fella at the doctor's office. What's that all about?"

"That fella was a boy named Ben Hodge. When Adams came to town, I hired Hodge to follow him. Apparently, he didn't do such a good job. Adams caught him."

"Did he tell him who he worked for?"

"No, but Adams followed Hodge to this building. Before the boy could get to me, he fell down the stairs and hit his head. He's been unconscious until today."

"Oh, I see," the man said. "So today he woke up and talked to Adams and probably gave him your name. Has Adams been here?"

"No," the man said.

"Why not?"

"All I can figure is that he's waiting for the judge to arrive so he can tell him."

"Why not the sheriff?"

"He doesn't trust the sheriff," the man said, "and with good reason. The sheriff works for me."

"So what do you want us to do?"

"I want you to get rid of Adams," the man said, "and it has to be tonight."

"Tonight?" Doyle said. "What if we're not ready?"

"I'll pay you more," the man said. Hell, he thought, this might end up costing him all of the money he'd stolen from Calamity Jane that night.

"All right, then," Doyle said, "we'll do it tonight. By tomorrow, you won't have any more worries."

As Doyle left, the man thought about the gunman's last words and doubted that they were true. Whatever years he had left in his life, he was sure they were going to be *full* of worries.

Marie Parsons was shopping when she heard the word that Clint Adams probably knew who had killed her husband—*if* it wasn't Calamity Jane, that is. Maybe all he had found out was that it *was* Calamity Jane that did it. If it wasn't, though, as both she and Clint agreed, then whoever was behind her husband's death was going to have to try to kill Clint, as well.

She certainly did not profess to love Clint Adams, not on such short acquaintance, but she had never before met a man who could match her in bed. It would be a shame for him to die before they had another chance to be together.

Mae Powers also heard the rumors. She was definitely angry at Clint Adams, but she certainly did not want him to die.

Besides, she needed him alive in order to get him back to her roulette wheel.

Clint knew that he'd just made doubly sure that there was a bull's-eye painted on his back. Whoever was behind the death of Parsons was going to have to make a move on him before the judge arrived. He figured today or tomorrow for sure.

He'd been in this situation before, and more often than not, on his own. Every so often he'd have somebody around that he could trust to watch his back, but the only man in town he *might* have been able to trust was Sam Teacher, and he was a gambler and a saloon owner, not a gunman. He was also not such good friends with Clint that he'd risk his life for him. More than likely Teacher would be rooting for him to come out of this alive, but that would be the extent of his support.

Once again, Clint knew, he was on his own and in the line of fire. He'd lived his whole life like this and had always known that this was the way it would end.

He just hoped that it wouldn't end here in Deadwood, where it had all ended for Wild Bill Hickok.

FORTY-SIX

Clint decided that night—after there had been no attempts on his life all day—that the best place to wait for it was the Dead Man's Hand Saloon. Somehow, even though he hoped that his fate would not be the same as Wild Bill Hickok's, that seemed the appropriate place to wait for it to happen—whatever *it* was.

He entered the saloon and found it extremely busy. Still, he was able to find a space at the bar that his body could fit into and ordered a beer from Nate. While he was drinking it, Sam Teacher came over. The patrons made room for the boss.

"Tempting fate, aren't you?"

The meaning of the remark was not lost on Clint.

"Maybe I'm trying to disprove something."

"Maybe," Teacher said. "While you're disproving it, do you think you could do something for me?"

"What?"

"The woman you said you wouldn't ruin on me has been sort of down in the mouth all day. Why don't you go over to the wheel and give her a chance to get my money back?"

"All six hundred?"

"Why not?" Teacher asked. "I gave you a chance, didn't I?"

Clint smiled.

"All on one number?"

"At thirty-seven to one?" Teacher said. "Do I look like a fool? No, the same bet you made last time."

"All on one color?"

"Right."

Clint thought a moment, then shrugged and said, "Why not?"

"Come on," Teacher said. "Pick up your beer. It's on the house."

Clint took up his beer mug and followed Teacher to the roulette wheel.

The patrons who saw them coming knew *why* they were coming and moved to give them both room.

"Come back for another try?" Mae asked Clint.

"I thought you were the one getting another try," he said.

"Either way," she said. "What's your bet?"

Clint thought about standing and watching the

wheel turn for a while, but he wasn't in the mood, and the six hundred dollars *was* just extra money. Whether he left town with it or not wasn't important. The important thing was that he lived to leave town.

Clint put his hand in his pocket for the money, which he was carrying with him tonight.

Teacher put his hand on Clint's arm.

"We trust you that it's there," he said. "Just call out a color."

"All right," Clint said. He looked at Mae and said, "Black, please."

"Place your bets," Mae said, but nobody else did. They all knew that Clint was playing double or nothing with six hundred dollars and they wanted to see how it came out.

Peripherally, Clint was aware of the batwing doors swinging open and three men entering the bar. He looked at Teacher, who looked past him and followed the men with his eyes.

Clint heard the wheel start to turn, and a moment later heard the ball start on its journey. He wasn't watching the wheel or the ball, though, he was watching Sam Teacher.

Matt Doyle entered the saloon with a man on either side of him.

"Spread out," he said. "He's at the roulette wheel. Move when I do."

The other two men moved away from him. For a moment Doyle thought of calling out to Clint Adams, but why give him that chance? There was a lot of money riding on this, and it wouldn't be

the first time somebody had been back-shot on
this spot.

He drew his gun. . . .

"Now!" Teacher shouted and dropped to the
floor.

Clint turned, drawing his gun at the same time,
dropping to one knee.

Doyle got off the first shot, but it went over
Clint's head. Clint fired and saw his bullet strike
the man in the right shoulder, high up. It spun
him around and caused him to drop his gun, but
Clint knew the shot wouldn't kill him. That was
good. He needed one of them alive to say who
had hired them.

Since he'd wounded the first man, there was no
need to be anything but deadly accurate with the
other two.

People were still hitting the floor, scraping back
chairs and overturning tables as Clint adjusted
and fired again. He hit the second man dead
square in the chest. The man's finger jerked on
the trigger and his shot went into the ceiling.

The third man fired, his shot missing Clint but
striking the roulette table. In fact, his bullet made
a hole in the number twenty-five.

Clint fired twice, just to make sure, and both
shots struck the man. Shot through the heart, the
gunman was dead before he hit the floor.

Clint knew that two of the men were dead and
one was wounded. It wouldn't be hard to get the
wounded one to talk and say who had hired him,
although Clint had a pretty good feeling the Gen-

eral was behind this. Calamity Jane was as good as cleared.

Suddenly, in the quiet that followed the shots, he became aware of the sound of the little ball bouncing around on the roulette wheel. He turned and looked at it just as it settled into a certain number. The number, however, did not matter. Only the color.

Mae, who had ducked under the table, stood up and looked down at the wheel. She looked up at Clint and smiled.

"Red," she said.

Sam Teacher got to his feet, looked at the wheel, and then looked at Clint.

Clint holstered his gun and said to both of them, "Well, you can't win them all."

Watch for

BLIND JUSTICE

147th novel in the exciting GUNSMITH series
from Jove

Coming in March!